CHAPTER 1

THE MORNING AWAITS

It was the early 1980s. Everything was different then; regarding customs and beliefs. It's always been a beautiful small Island, surrounded by the Caribbean Sea – Jamaica. The blue seas and white' sands, combined with its tropical weather and it's many other amazing attractions. In one of its parishes, Manchester, was a small district called Sawyer Town, surrounded by tall pine trees, and acres and acres of farm land. There lived a family: John their father, Ms Jane his wife and their eight children.

Early mornings felt like it was midday, as the sun rose into the skies, taking its position of choice. Glaring through the windowpane, the curtains were its protector but were no match, not even close enough to hold it back. The dogs were barking, overjoyed to see the crack of dawn, while the rooster flew to a high of contentment. Spreading his bedazzling feathers, stretching his neck like a swan. Cock a-doodle-doo, was the melody of his song; every morning would be the same – Oh! this must be Groundhog Day, thought Rose. Stepping outside, you could feel the fresh air caressing your skin, sending chills down your spine, embracing a combination of both worlds. "Time for school, children," their mother would call out to Rose and her siblings. You could hear her coming through the hall, dragging her bed slippers along the floor behind her, sounding like she wasn't lifting her feet."

Wake up, wake up, you need to go fetch water from the spring and fill the drums, before you leave for school", she shouted at them. Rose and the others had to make sure that they did their chores before they left each day. That was the norm for them every morning, even though Rose didn't like it. She much preferred the evening time.

The pathway that led to the spring bed was, at times, slippery and damp due to overnight dew. The path was narrow, and also filled with tiny thorns that would pierce through your skin, if you weren't careful. Rose and her brother walked past a huge mango tree, that had been there for centuries but never seemed to bear any fruit. They believed that the water came from under the ground, no one knew its true origin; it flows up from the ground, unique and mysterious.

"Hurry up or you`ll be late for school, I don't know why you didn't fill the drums yesterday," Rose's mother said, looking annoyed. Rose glanced in her mother's direction and then she said, "but mama, we went to the spring yesterday, and poured water into the drum." Her mother, rolled her eyes.

"Stop talking and go".

"Yes, mama," "she grinned. It wasn't worth the beating. It was best just to obey and stop wasting time. Well, Rose and Willy. her brother, had the most responsibilities. Willy was older than Rose, but was the youngest of the three brothers. It was up to them to be productive and so off they went. Del would stay back and wash the dishes. She would often pretend to be feeling unwell; that was her way of escaping her chores. "Mama I'm not feeling well," she said, hoping for sympathy, but mama knew her all too well." Child go and wash the dishes", their mother would yell at her. "Ok, mama I'm going to do it now, she would mumble under her breath, still pretending about how ill she was feeling.

2

The Matchstick that Kept Burning

Paulette Graham

The Matchstick that Kept Burning

Copyright © 2021 Paulette Graham

ISBN:
978-1-80227-133-1 (Paperback)
978-1-80227-134-8 (eBook)

"An inspiring read which is both invigorating and captivating. It depicts the real essence of trying your best to improve and be supportive to others."

~ Mitchelle Victoria (NHS Nurse)

"*The Matchstick That Kept Burning*, is a refreshing and detailed memoir. It embarked on Rose's journey and struggles as a young girl and her triumph and ability to overcome, beating all odds. Filled with humor, suspense, and drama...... It's an utter must-read."

~ Christine Green (Autism Carer)

"The book is refreshing as the reader was able to see the book through, the writers' eyes. The challenges that made her who she is, this book shows that once you're determined, you'll receive what you want through hard work."

~ Nicholas Haze (University Student)

"Having gone through my own struggles, the book has opened my eyes about a young girl's journey. With determination and motivation, she rises above it all making what seems impossible, possible. It's a must-read."

~ Diana Nyamu Danda (Student)

Contents

1. THE MORNING AWAITS   1

2. THE EARLIER YEARS   19

3. THE BEGINING OF THE DARK DAYS   39

4. The JOURNEY TO CLARENDON   57

5. THE UNKNOWN CITY   72

6. MOVING INTO THE SLUM   95

7. THE UNDISCOVER SONGBIRD   118

8. A NEW WORLD OF MOTHERHOOD   138

9. DECISION TIME, NO RETURN   157

10. A TRIP TO THE FOREIGN LAND   177

11. THE BEGINING AND THE END   194

12. WHERE ARE THEY NOW   210

"What did you say"? their mother asked Del.

"Nothing mama. I didn't say anything", she said, walking off to wash the dishes, clearly displaying her disappointment. "Remember Rose," her mother added, "when you return home this evening you'll fetch water from the spring and refill the drums again". Rose's mom, Ms Jane, had a lot to do regarding using the supply of water but they already knew that she was in a right mood, Rose thought to herself. Jena was the youngest, so she got away with most of the chores during the morning hours; apart from being the youngest, most of the time she wasn't well enough to help. She would put her uniform on before everyone else. She was like a delicate flower due to her asthmatic condition and was frequently unwell. As a child her favourite drink was milo tea, or sometimes milk; that was all she demanded. Mama used to try her best, making sure she had both in the house. Rose was protective of Jena, but she wasn't the only one; it was the same with all the inhabitants of the house. The asthmatic attacks were severe and at times wore heavily upon her tiny frame; it was difficult knowing if she would survive, but somehow she did. Rose's mother always knew what to do to get Jena back on her feet, even through her worse days when Rose, and the others, would be screaming that she was dying. Ms Jane had to rush off to the hospital in a panic, probably crying her eyes out over the tiny frame.

Rose had three brothers and four sisters, so including herself there were eight of them altogether. Tom was the oldest, followed by Joe and the Verna, the oldest sister. Maria came after her, then Willy, with Rose next in line. Del followed and Jenna was the youngest. Del was chubby and short, amusing and fun, she always had some jokes up her sleeve, or was playing tricks on whoever was available. She, too, suffered from poor health; the doctors believed she had a hole in her heart (the medical term for the condition was 'atrial septal defect') but it was never severe. However, that didn't stop her from being the troublesome one. She would get herself into the worst situation with her siblings, but then use her heart condition to get out of it. Rose was sometimes annoyed with her behaviour and would sometimes give her a set down, often defending Jena`s honour - the poor little thing was frightened of Del. They were like normal siblings, fighting now and then. Playing together was always something they enjoyed. They had no other technology or gadgets.

Rose and her sisters invented their own games. Rope skipping was fun, I want to go first," demanded Del, looking excited. Rose stared at her, surprised.

"Why do you think you`ll be first?" Jena asked Del, sounding annoyed as she kept on biting her nails. You could tell she was hoping Rose might say something!

"Del you won't be going first today. Every time you do the same thing," Rose interrupted her, before she had a chance to say anything else." I`m not joking with you", Rose, continued. "Jena, is right," and in that instant Del looked defeated, but wouldn't dare argue but instead, she took the other end of the rope gladly.

"Is second alright Rose?" she asked timidly.

"Yes, that's fine by me", Rose replied, nodding her head in agreement. She could see Jena was pleased to be allowed to take the first turn at skipping, today. They`ll all get their turns, as they laughed and joked around.

Rose's yard had some unusual plants and flowers, right at the front where everyone could see them. The pine tree with its arch shape, was cut to perfection. Then, one day while it was raining, and hail was beating down upon the ground like an ice storm, the thunder rolling like the master of many roars, when suddenly the lightening came flashing with a vengeance, striking the pine tree almost in half.

"Thank God," Rose's mother said, "no one was standing under the tree at the time, otherwise they would be struck down dead".

There` were a few palm trees, with some fine cutting edges, in the form of a gate, surrounding the half pyramid of their house, blocking out peering eyes. Rose's mother, who took great pride in her flower beds, had never seen such beauty: different colours, shapes, she had it all. It was like walking through the forbidden garden, she was the only one who could give away plants, and that wasn't often. She even had pots of flowers on the outside under her bedroom window. Rose, and her sisters always thought it was a good idea, considering how low the windows of the house were made. It was too transparent, 'as clear as glass' so the old saying goes. They never had regular toys, no dolls, or girlie objects, not that they weren't allowed. Rose's parents believed that their money could be better spent on things of more value, like sending them to school. Rose had two younger sisters and her brother, included herself, going to school at that time, so there wasn't much to spare. They had imaginary friends, which was quite normal, plus they knew how to be creative. Back then marble games were mostly for boys, but Rose and her sisters knew how to play with other makeshift toys. They would gather the corn silks from the fields and play with them in place of dolls. They would add a tiny piece of cloth to the golden silk, pretending it was a ribbon. How sad, you might think, but for them it was fun and laughter.

The journey to primary school was like walking a marathon, running too, considering thirteen miles on foot, if they decided to walk on the main road. While walking through the forest was a shorter distance, about seven miles, still it wasn't like licking an ice cream cone.

But their choices were limited, and god knows, neither was better but they could either walk and save a few pennies to buy lunch, or they could go hungry and take the bus. The forest was filled with pine trees, and it was like visiting the witch's hut in the Hansel and Gretel story. The hills were steep to climb, and when it rained the day before, it would be worse for them. Willy was protective of his sisters, making sure that they were safe whenever he was around.

"Rose, he shouted! "We've got to leave now, remember the sun is rising, it's going to be warmer soon". To get to school on time, they had to wake up early in the mornings. Even the sounds of the night crickets chirping nearby could still be heard. They all would leave home together; "we can't take the bus this morning otherwise, we won't have enough money left for food," he told them. Rose looked at Jena and Del, could see how disappointed they were, but kept quiet.

"Come on let's go," said Rose," as they walked towards the old stone road, from their house. They kept walking, until they got to the main road, which seemed to be well made, laced in black tar. For as long as they could remember, whenever it got hot, they could smell the odour , flowing through the air; a dirty ,gritty scent that never seemed to go away. Rose and the others were saying good morning, to basically everyone they met. If they didn't their parents would surely hear about it. A few more minutes to go, not far now, and looking ahead they saw a small wooden hut under the hill. As they continued to move closer to the edge of the forest, it seemed relentless; the pine trees were tall, bending, and adjoined, like they were communicating in whispers.

They had now left the main road. As they continued their journey through the forest, the path was narrow and steep, and the ground was of red clay dirt but was together almost moist. Rose began to move slowly with much carefulness, in the hope of not slipping. She held her sister's hands as they started climbing the slope, and by the time they got to the top, Jena's breathing became unsteady leaving her nearly breathless. Willy took Jena's arm from Rose; he was now walking at a slower pace, but it didn't help much. He then knelt on the ground and told her to climb onto his back and he proceeded to carry her. She was getting worse and her crying wasn't making her condition any better. Willy became frightened and so did everyone else.

"I have to take her back home," he said with great concern."

"Yes, you`ll have to. Mama knows what to do," Rose replied. f please don't let her die on us – Rose`s thoughts were going into overdrive, and she could see that they were all scared. Willy and Rose decided that it was best for Willy to take her back home, and as she was unable to walk he would have to carry her on his back. Rose and Del would carry on to school. The sun was getting hotter, beating down upon their bodies.

"Do you think she`ll be ok"? Del asked Rose. She was miles away, deep in thoughts and because of that, she didn't hear what her sister was saying. "Can you please answer me," she begged, seemly confused.

"Sorry Del," Rose, replied, "what did you say?"

She then repeated herself, "I said do you believe Jena, will be alright?" her voice filled with emotion, Rose glanced at her face. "Listen Del", she nodded her head and continued to reassure her sister, "Oh yes! mama is going to make her better. When we get home, you`ll see, she will be as good as new".

The sun was now shining down in all its brightness and heat, and they were sweating mildly under their armpits. The rest of their journey was mostly in silence, although now and then Rose would say something to check that Del was OK. When they got home from school that day Jena was lying in bed, but was looking better than when they last saw her. The next few years of primary school Jena hardly attended due to her illness but when she got the chance, she was brilliant at it. By the time she was old enough to attend high school her asthma condition reduced to an incredible level, making her more active and healthier. Whenever the weather changed, even though it`s a tropical country, it would feel cooler sometimes, especially nearer to Christmas, and that was when Jena, would become ill.

Whenever, it rained it would seem almost impossible to achieve anything other than a hazardous outcome; Rose and the others would have to remove their wet school shoes, carrying them in their hands unless they didn't need to wear them the following day. As they struggled to find their grip on the ground, Rose and her sisters were disgusted by the sodden mud accumulating between their toes.

"Oh my God!" Del shouted, "I`m going to fall,".

"Sorry," Rose replied, "I can't help much. I can't find a suitable spot to put my own feet down. Try coming closer towards me," I'll dig bigger holes in the ground with my feet. Just put your feet in my footsteps. Follow my lead," Rose reassured her. Del wasn't complaining so much anymore, and Rose thought to herself, 'thank God for small mercies'. Rose smiled reassuringly at her sister as they continued down the steep hill. The hardest work was for Willy; if Jena was there, it was his duty to keep her safe, Rose had to carry their school bags, but that was the least she could do. On a few occasions, Rose or one of the others would fall over, leaving no room for anything else but the mud, and probably dog poo, too, if the truth be known, looking as if they were buried alive in the mud. There was only one bus that operated for the entire area, including all the outlying communities. It was really designed to carry adults, and keep in mind that they (the adults) were always given priority, don't think for a moment that you would be seated unless the old blue bus had no adults on. If you're holding your breath for that to happened, surely you might die in the process. Even so, they were often packed like sardines in a tin, filled with sweaty armpits and foul body odour, pushing you back and forth. It was better walking, but to avoid the treacherous journey through the forest after the rain, walking the long way home was their only choice and salvation, when they had no money left to spare. There were plenty of others who were far shabbier than Rose and her siblings; for everyone it was an everyday struggle.

Occasionally, whenever they were extra late for school, Rose and her siblings would stop at a house that belonged to a friend of their father, until it was lunch time; then they would sneak onto the school premises. No one ever really noticed except a few of their particular friends who would normally behave as if they had been there all the time. Mobile phones were non-existent at that time, making communication almost impossible, so they could give the teachers any excuse that they came up with about their lateness.

Rose was a loner; never had a lot of friends during her school years but was friendly enough to stay visible. Willy was the popular one. Almost everyone knew him. He took part in all the sports activities and was friends with the elite groups of boys. He was very chatty, always talking a lot, especially around his friends. Del wasn't such a confident person; sometimes she felt intimidated because of her weight issues, but she, too, knew how to survive in a world of unpleasantness. As a child you held in the hurt and pain that others inflicted on you. When the hurt was too much to bear, then inevitably you will unleash your anger upon them, anticipating the moment, until the right time comes along. Rose didn't like school very much, especially in her earlier years, and got into a few fights after been bullied too often. She was generally too afraid to defend her honour, until one day she wasn't afraid anymore. Eventually the bullying stopped that's when she told herself, that she wouldn't allow herself to be weak and afraid anymore.

Rose and her sisters were expected to maintain certain principles, and that was to learn the domestic arts of washing, cooking and keeping the house clean; these were their priorities, even if they were unable to do anything else. That was a massive accomplishment. Rose was cooking for the entire family at the age of thirteen; her mother taught them all the best way she could. Rose was a soup specialist, at least that was what her papa would say to the others, when he was in a one of his OK moods. She felt proud of herself, as she was never usually given much admiration for anything, but that was typical for them. Friday was the great soup day, and Rose would be in the kitchen preparing the ingredients that she needed. Cutting the meat and vegetables, she sometimes thought of herself as a young chef, but that was merely daydreaming. Her mother would be nearby, in case she needed any assistance. The old metal pot sitting on the fire stones ready for action, was as black as midnight.

The interior was shiny like a silver spoon, but regardless of all its shining glory, its only purpose was for cooking. The kitchen was built separately, from the house having its own structure. It was small, half the size of a bedroom, with a tiny window and an entrance door to it. Those days, having gas stoves wasn't affordable for anyone in the community. Inside, the kitchen the fireplace had three large stones that kept the pot in place. Dry firewood was used for the cooking. The smoke would escape through the air, slowly drifting away. It was making Rose's eyes water, so that she could hardly see anything, but after time passed, she learned how to tolerate the smoke, when cooking in the kitchen. After Rose, had finished the cooking she would place the dishes on the table to serve the meal to everyone.

"Mama," she called out, please come and help me with the serving."

"Ok, Rose, I'm coming," her mother would respond in a distracted manner form somewhere from the front of the house. "This soup looks and smells delicious," her mother would say with much approval. Rose would smile, feeling happy about herself, as she carried the food inside the house for her mother to serve, calling out everyone's name as she placed it on the dinner table. They all came, appearing to be half starved.

"Thanks Rose," they said, taking their plates from the table. No one really bothered to sit at the table, except Roses' father. It was common practice to eat wherever they choose. After dinner, Del would do the washing up, and sometimes Jena would help her with the packing away.

They had no running water in the house so Rose and her sisters had two choices; either carrying, enough water to wash their clothing at home, or going to the riverbed to do it. They'd do the washing for almost everyone who lived in the house. Doing the washing at home seemed to take forever. It would all go into that old metal bath pan, and be scrubbed clean on the wooden washing board, placed in the middle of the tub, scrubbing away like your life depended upon it, making sure that every last bit of that garment was as clean as possible. The sun would have no mercy on them as it, burst through the branches of the shady tree, like a storm. 'Well, what would I give not to go down to that riverbed,' Rose, thought to herself, 'but making that many trips, carrying that water would surely rip the hair from our scalps. I sure couldn't imagine what we would look like. Probably like some of those bald-headed hens running around in the yard!. Rose was unable hold back the laughter. As Del came around the corner of the house she saw

11

Rose looking quiet amused staring at the chickens flopping around. She stood there just watching Rose, as if she expected something bizarre to happened.

"What're you doing Rose?" her sister asked, inquisitively.

"Nothing really, "Rose responded.

"I bet you're probably talking to those chickens," Rose's sister continued. Rose looked at her, laughing even harder, then she said, "you had to spoil the joke didn't you?. I'm not going to tell you now". Del didn't seem to care as she walk away. The following day Rose's mother packed the bath pan with the dirty clothing, and handed her the washing soap. Del, too, had her pile of clothing ready to put on her head to carry, seemly exhausted even before she reached the riverbed. As Rose and her sister balanced the pan of clothing on their heads, they were off.

"I hope nobody is at the river today," Del, whispered, "you know what it's like whenever our cousins get there before us".

Rose and her sister had to travel through their uncle's yard to get to the river. Most of their cousins from their mothers' side of the family were living there, close to each other. He was there, their favourite uncle from their mother's side. Tall as an ostrich, and just a tiny bit bent, he was the funniest person they knew. His wife was Rose's best friend's mother, and she too was a lovely, kind person. She could be boastful and outspoken when she wanted to be, but was never malicious about her actions. She treated Rose and her siblings well.

"Good morning, aunty", they greeted her. This was a form of respect, even though she wasn't their blood relative.

"How're you children doing today"?

"We`re alright," Rose and her sister would reply. "So, did you see anyone go down by the river to do their washing, today?" Rose asked her shyly.

"No. I haven't seen anyone," she'd answer. But listen. I`ll save you some lunch for when you get back."

"Oh, thank you, Ms Will." She was a good cook, one of a select few. Their parents taught them not to consume food that was given to them by certain people, and some were not what they seemed to be, but Ms Will was an exception. It was nice how she treated them, but with her there was always some sort of drama going on. If she was a news reporter she would surely be famous. Rose hadn't met anyone who exaggerated in such a manner. Others believed that she was too overbearing, but there were still a few who did admire her. Apart from her unrequired behaviour, she had good qualities too, that Rose and her siblings at times found hilarious.

The earlier they got going to the riverbed, the better it was for them, because the sun`s fury wasn't going to wait. They hurried down the hill towards the riverbed.

"Please, slow down. Wait for me Rose," her sister would say, as she tried to catch up. Rose slowed down her pace, until Del got closer. Nothing was ever great about going down a sloping hill, often falling over on your ass. They'd finally get to the river.

"Oh yes! We`re the first ones here," her sister smiled as she slowly moved towards the water. Everything looked so fierce, you had to be careful or the water would sweep the clothing away. At least there was plenty of water at their disposal, and enough rocks to scrub away the dirt from the clothing. You could hear echoes from all around, of animals and people, the crickets, too, wouldn't keep silent, birds were singing.

"Remember when Verna and Maria used to do the washing?" Rose reminded her sister.

"Yes, I do," Del answered. "You mean those days when we used to help carry the clothing home. We had to make so many journey`s back and forth, due to the amount of clothing they had to wash."

"Ha!" Rose was laughing so hard, she couldn't complete her sentence. "Honestly" she managed to say, "I thought we would be bald headed before we turned fifteen, our heads are like donkeys from carrying the loads".

"My goodness, Rose," said Del, "your imagination is beyond this world, but I believe you're right." They would sit down, chatting about things of the past, the laughter was so contaminating, that even if you were a horse, you would be giggling, too.

"Oh, yes how could I forget", Rose's sister answered, then she proceeded to do her own reminiscing. "Remember that time when we were almost at the top of the hill, and suddenly I slipped and fell. The pan of clothing got really spoilt and covered in dirt."

Rose laughed so hard, she was unable to make sense; they were both laughing so much they thought their sides would split.

"Well, you were rolling like some breadfruit," Rose, said jokingly, but suddenly Del, wasn't finding that hilarious anymore. The expression on her face changed into a half embarrassed smile.

"Come now Del. It's just you and me, no one else is here, You often say silly things to me, but I never cried."

"But what if someone was coming and heard you?" her sister replied, looking uneasy.

"Ok, stop being so over dramatic," said Rose and with that she changed the subject. Rose realized that due to Del's weight, her sister had taken offense and she didn't wish to keep talking about it.

"I`m tired," Del, started complaining. Rose glanced at her without responding. The sun was now getting hotter, beating down on their backs like fire balls.

"I'll wash the larger pieces of clothing, while you wash the smaller ones," Rose said ,as she took the clothing from her sister. Del appeared to look less tired as she hummed away to herself, as she scrubbed the cloth against the rock.

It was almost lunch time, and Rose wasn't speaking anymore. She went quiet, focusing on the task ahead. Being the oldest comes with great responsibilities and she was aware of that. Another hour passed, and Rose and her sister were now packing up the wet clothing, as they were finishing for the day.

Their hindrance was standing in front of them; that steep old red dirt hill, that had no mercy or sympathy, was always ready to cause havoc. Rose wasn't prepared to wash twice, for every problem there`s a solution her mother used to say. The pathway, that lead around the hill was much more time consuming but was safer. Rose explained the situation to her sister, who didn't seem to mind. "Follow closely," Rose told her. The pathway had a few thorns hovering along its edges, so they had to be careful. Eventually they were at the top of the hill, looking down into the river. There were some people on the other side of the hill attending to their animals: cows and goats. It was obvious that the animals, were been fed in the grass meadow as was quite common. As they climbed the hill, toward their uncle's house, Rose felt her knees shaking but she kept pushing forward. 'I need to sit down for a minute' Rose thought to herself, as she hesitated under a big, shady pine tree, and looked all around her in dismay.

Eventually she took the pan of wet clothes off her head, and assisted her sister to do the same. Del seemed relieved that they were able to rest.

"Rose," she said, I was just about to beg you to stop. I'm so hungry and tired".

Hah! Rose felt sympathy towards her, even though she too was exhausted. As they sat under a tree, they could feel the breeze blowing in their direction, even though the sun was still at its hottest. The shade from the tree was now disappearing.

"Come on, let's go," Rose said relentlessly. "Maybe we`ll get something to eat when we get to our uncle's house."

"Remember Ms Will told us this morning that she would leave us some lunch for when we returned," Rose's sister reminded her. At the mention of food, Rose opened her eyes a little wider.

"Oh, yeh! I almost forgot," she answered.

"Really? You?" Del asked eyeballing Rose closely.

"Not today Del. I'm too tired to be bothered by you now", she said, giving her the glimmer of a smile ."We`ll be there soon," she continued, then said, "Wonder what she cooked today? I hope it's white rice with curry chicken. Boy, I can taste it on my lips already". You could tell by her enthusiasm how excited she was.

" Just be careful," Rose disrupted her food fest daydream., "Del, I wouldn't like to see you fall over," she went on to say. There`s nothing to prevent you from rolling right down that horrible riverbed. Rose was exaggerating. She knew how scared her sister was of falling and just needed her to stop talking. They could now see the house. They could see Ms Will speaking to someone in the yard. Her voice was energetic and loud; some people said she had a deafeningly voice. She saw Rose and her sister coming towards her, with the pans of clothing on their heads.

"My goodness," she greeted them. "I was wondering if maybe you had already passed by, and I didn't see you girls.

They weren't sure as to why she might think that. Del had a disappointed expression on her face. "Take the pans off your heads and rest for a while," she told them. They obeyed her request, and did what she asked. Rose thought that maybe there was no food, but surprisingly Ms Will went into her kitchen and came out with two plates of food. They were grateful and ate until their hearts were content.

"Thanks Ms Will", they both said, looking at each other. Oh, it was a good day, and the food tasted delicious. She then came back and gave them each a cup of lemonade. It was delightful and quenched their thirst beautifully. Rose and Del were so relieved that all their tiredness suddenly disappeared. They always enjoyed Ms Will cooking. As they were about to leave, their uncle came into the yard. He was coming from his vineyard, smiling from cheek to cheek.

"Hello girls", he greeted them.

"Hi uncle", they answered politely, but there wasn't enough time to chit chat; it was time to go home.

They said their goodbyes to their uncle and his wife, and off they went. With a full belly, and in a happier mood Rose and her sister were talking and laughing throughout the rest of their journey. On their way home they passed several houses but luckily for them their route wasn't on the main road. 'Ha, I would have died of embarrassment,' Rose imagined. When they got home their mother was in the kitchen preparing dinner. When she heard Rose and Del, she came out of the kitchen.

"Never knew that you girls, were coming back," she protested.

"But mama," Del said, "It was a lot of clothes, plus the sun was really hot on our bodies". On that note, it was unlikely she was in the mood to argue. Instead, she just nodded her head.

"Come on then, so I can hang the clothing on the line before the sun goes down."

She ushered them in. Rose stayed back to help her, while Del walked away looking for Jena. Rose observed her mother`s mood seemed a little off. 'It couldn't have been us staying longer than usually, surely. We`ve done this before. It must be something else that's making her so distant,' Rose thought to herself. She wasn't one to show sadness. If that did happen then it would be a call for concern.

"Mama! Are you doing alright?" Rose gathered her courage and asked her. She didn't answer, just kept hanging the clothing. Clearly chatting wasn't on her mind. Minutes later, she mumbled something about Rose`s dad. She then realised the dismal mood her mother was in, leaving her with a daunted feeling in her mind.

Chapter 2
THE EARLIER YEARS

They seemed like a regular family, and they were, but there was more to their lives than, at first, met the eye; it was incredibly challenging. The atmosphere was unbalanced, sad and daunting to be around, let alone living in it. Rose, and her siblings lived in a three-bedroom house that had an open plan living and dining hall, that was the most attractive part of the house. It had a veranda attached to the front of the house facing the street, anyone to who was going about their journey, the inhabitants would be exposed for all to see; there was nowhere to hide. During the year of 1980, the inhabitants in the community had no television to inform them of what was happening in the world; radios were the only source that they had. Rose's dad had a brother, who had migrated to Canada with his family, but he would return almost every year. It so happened on one of his visits, he brought back a black and white television for Rose`s dad. When the television came to the house everyone was overly excited, especially Rose and her siblings. They were acting like mice around cheese. Everyone was curious as to how it would work, considering it had no instruction manual, so that was something to watch.

Rose's dad thought that he would be a hero and show how smart he was, but that didn't work out for him; the result was far from accomplishing his goal.

"Yeah," he said looking defeated, one of you children, come and search for the television channels, I don't really understand the remote". Jena was the youngest, but she was a smart little thing, she stood up with confidence and said,

"OK papa, I can do it."

He looked at her in surprise. "Do you know what to do?" he asked her with interest. "Yes," she responded, and with that he handed her the remote. Her tiny finger was moving as if she was born to do it.

"Do you even know what you`re doing?" Rose interrupted her sister.

"Yes," Jena answered timidly.

"Leave her alone so she can focus," Rose's mother said, joking. In the next few minutes the TV was ready to go; both the channels were working (at that time there were only two). Jena, was crowned queen of the remote, and you could see how happy she was; everyone was very impressed, especially as she was the youngest in the family.

Words spread fast, good ones and bad, and soon everyone in the neighbourhood knew about their television set. Their uncle, from Rose`s mother's side of the family, was good friends with Rose`s dad, so every evening he was there, at the house. They all liked having him around; he was funny and witty. It became a spectacular moment for them, the first family to own a tv set, and their neighbours, and others living in the wider community, soon came to scrutinize the new discovery. It felt like having a new toy, and all the children wanted to play with it. Except these weren't children alone, but their parents, too. It gave the children a wonderful feeling of self-importance. On weekends Rose's house would be filled with children, mostly cousins; it was like a mini-cinema. Oh, they were high in spirits and excitement. The house was filled with chattery and whispers before the Sunday matinee or movie began. Soon there would be silence, and you wouldn't be able to hear a straw if it fell to the floor. The martinis would last for over an hour, their piercing eyes were glued to the television set, and that would be the best highlight of the day. Rose and her cousins lived just a stone's throw away from each other, so it didn't require any transport for them to get there, and many arrived well before the show began, finding a comfortably seat was important for them.

The expressions on their faces were priceless; after the film was over, they would be talking about it for days on end. It was amusing how everyone would fall into character, imitating their favourite actor, or actions. Running in slow motion and jumping over hoops, rolling on the ground like they were tyres. When it was time for them to go home, they would be anticipating the following week ahead; it was all they talked about. Ms Jane, Rose`s mom, would be busy, handing out her baked pudding, made of cornmeal and sweet potatoes with added spices. After all that excitement, it was clear that they need something. The evenings were still bright, so they decided on staying longer. Rose's mother was eager for them to get home safely and in good time.

"It`s time to go home, children. It'll be dark soon, " she told them.

"OK, auntie," they'd respond.

"See you children next week. Walk good," she waved at them.

Rose and her siblings would often be sitting on the veranda in the evening, watching the sunset as it went down in the West. It seemed that wasn't the only thing that they would actually be watching; Rose and her sisters would gaze at vehicles and people going by, like chickens in a barnyard. Their most remarkable time together was when they were hanging out, sharing the same common goals, laughing at each other's jokes. They made each other feel safe; some of their bonds were unbreakable even though individually they were all different. Jena and Del's sense of humour was magical, best sisters ever, and Rose loved them dearly. The area was a quiet place to live, miles of bushes as far as the eyes could see; just crops and plants. The people were living within close proximity of each other; a scream or an argument, it wouldn't be hard to trace the source, especially in the still of the night. Some of the neighbours were nosy and gossiped like teenagers on spring break, while others would attend to their own business and kept to themselves or so they led you to believe.

However, the house that Rose lived in was often very unbalanced; there was always an intensity about what was going to happened next. They had a strict upbringing; even when visiting families and friends, they had to be back home before it turned dark. Rose`s mother would occasionally take the children to church on Saturdays, which was their Sabbath day. Rose, along with her brothers and sisters, all grew up in the same household, and had the same mom and dad. Rose`s dad was loved by some and hated by a few in his community, but he was a reliable farmer. The people who brought his crop could depend on him coming through , and almost everyone knew him. He was a farmer; he cultivated large fields of yams and other food groups for a living. He had acres of lands that were just pure yam fields. People thought that he was financially stable, because he had more yam farms than everyone else in the community. Sadly, due to his bad habits it wasn't so. . He was a private person, leaving people to make their own assumptions about him, except what they saw for themself. Some were more negative than others. Even though he worked harder than anyone they knew it was excruciating to see how little he had. At times you could see him trying to figure out his predicament; that seemed almost impossible to comprehend.

He had employees working for him on his farms; he treated them very well and so, in return, they showed him their loyalty. They spoke about him as if he were the king of the land and of course he was their saviour. Rose`s mother and father got married very young; she was only nineteen, and he was just twenty-one, practically still young enough to be living home with their parents. However, instead, they were already living in their marital home. Rose was keen to understood why she got married at such a young age but was waiting for the appropriate moment. Eventually Rose found the courage to ask. Her mother was sitting on the veranda combing Jenna's hair; honestly, she wasn't the greatest stylist when it came to combing hair, but she did her best. Rose smiled, as she walked slowly towards her mother.

"Why`re you smiling, like when the cat's stealing the butter?" she said facetiously, still focusing on Jenna's hair."

" I just, need to ask you something mama." Rose hesitated.

"Oh," she said. Now looking at her, Rose was wishing that she had never mentioned it.

"Come now, what is it, Rose"?

Being the thinker, she wondered, 'what have I got to lose?'

"Why did you got married so young? Weren't you scared?" it finally came out.

Her mother seemed surprised but Rose could observe that she was ready to chat.

Rose's mother looked away from her for a brief second, and so she kept staring at her, watching for a reaction, hoping she would say something. Rose felt a sudden sadness towards her. Her mother nodded her head, in despair and replied,

"Yes, I was especially scared of the unknown." She continued, "Yeah, when we first moved here, it was extremely hard for us at times. After we got married, and moved into the community, there wasn't always enough to feed us all. At that time it was just Tom, Joe Verna and Maria, your father and myself but the little that we did have, we shared it with everyone. The house was only a one bedroom, a bathroom, and a small living hall; it was nothing like it is now. Refrigerators in those days were only for people who could afford it, not for people like us." Still looking cheerful as daylight she continued, "In order to keep our meat safe from being spoilt, we had to marinade it using plenty of salt and pimento seeds".

Rose's older sister, Maria, shouted,

"Oh yes, I used to help you, mama".

She nodded her head in agreement. "Even now we still do the same thing," Ms Jane, said. She was keen to explain to the children how things were, and still are. Rose and her younger siblings often saw meats hanging in one corner of the kitchen, over the fireplace. The smoke would be dancing, covering over the meat like a coat on a rainy day. Now they realised it was there, preserving. As the years went by Rose's dad would ask his sister, Aunt Clare, to store their meat in her fridge, until he finally brought one for his own household.

Rose and her siblings were familiar with the pigs being slaughtered; sometimes it would be a goat but that would be rarely, because that meat was way too expensive then. Chicken meat was only on Sundays, so that was Rose and her siblings' favourites day of the week. It was early morning, the dew was still lying on the grass, the flowers were blooming beautifully, in all their radiance. Rose's dad had three pigs in the pigpen; the oldest was about to be slaughtered. A tall slender man came in the yard, walking slowly, looking like a turtle on a rainy day. His voice was just above a whisper, when he spoke; surely there should be someone else assisting him. Rose stood there noticing his every move, wondering if he were even strong enough for the task at hand.

"I bet the pig would've probably bitten his hands off if he tried to do it on his own," she said to her youngest sister, Jena, looking at the man as they both burst out laughing. Jena was laughing so hard, it became funnier than ever. Rose held her sister's hands, pulling her away. Muttering to Jenna she said,

"the man is looking at us".

He turned around slowly to watch what was happening behind him, wondering why Rose and her sister were giggling so much.

"Girls, are you alright? Come, share the joke with me. I'd like a laugh too," he repeated himself, stammering through his sentences. They could tell he was acting discomfited, smiling crookedly as he leaned on the kitchen door. The lining of his face appeared to be bony, with visible lines across his forehead; he had obviously had a hard life. Rose looked quickly at him and then walked away towards the house.

Rose's dad was already preparing the place for the poor animal's demise; everyone seemed excited about the whole thing, even those that were ordering meat beforehand. The tall man walked towards the pigpen, with two other men behind him, they seemed to be ready for the kill. They threw a rope around the animal's neck, dragging and pulling it away with no regards.

I swear the pig was going to have a heart attack," Rose, said to her sister.

The pig was grunting for help; it must have been deeply distressed, what with all that resistance it was putting up. Eventually it was useless for him to keep trying, there was no escape. The more it struggled the less they seemed to care. Rose and her siblings were scared then, so they hid until the slaughter were over. The pig was skinned, cut into portions, then sold out to the customers who were waiting to consume the animal meat.

The children gazed at each other in dismay, and then positioned their sight on their mother. She saw how worried their faces were, so she immediately changed the topic to something more cheerful; you could see that she was really trying.

Rose and her siblings refer to their mother as mama, and their father, papa. By the time she had reached her forties, poor mama already had all her children. Her body had no time for recuperation, after giving birth to nine children (one of whom died during the process), above everything else that she went through. Rose's siblings were two to three years apart, so that couldn't have been a walk in the park for her; under the circumstances most people would not survive. Instead, she held on for the well-being of her children and herself.

"Rose," she asked, "what do you want to know".

Rose, anxiously pressed her thumb against the kitchen wall, clearing her throat she asked,

"Why did you stay with papa?".

Rose's mother looked at her oddly.

"My dear child when you get older and start having your own children, you will know," she said, smiling nervously.

Rose was not surprised about the answer given by her mother, even though she did not fully understand. "OK, mama" she responded walking off towards the house.

26

Anyway, as a farmer's wife, one of her responsibilities was preparing meals daily for the men that worked on the farm. Rose's dad had several farms, so it could be anywhere, close to home or far away. The meal would be prepared on an outside fire, built on three large stones, by the men working on the farm, or sometimes Ms Jane. The heat from the sun with the combination of the fire, would often feel like a furnace burning outside. In those conditions drinking plenty of water would be your only salvation, should you not have died from dehydration. Rose's dad was uneducated, so farming was all he knew and after years of experience, it became his finest art, one that he was good at. But even though he worked hard, he squandered his money away.

Ms Jane learnt the technique of sewing clothing, especially for the children; their school uniforms were most important. It was a matter of either paying someone to have it made or learning how to do it herself and with the little money she had to feed them all, she had little choice. She bore nine children, but sadly one passed way during birth. Rose's mother would sometimes say, "God knows best, he is in control all the time". She used that phase so often, and as a child it was hard to understand its meaning but as Rose got older, she understood.

Ms Jane had a lovely caramel complexion, and was always light-hearted no matter what life had thrown at her. She was taller than Rose's dad. Her jokes were spontaneous, and it was natural for her to get you laughing so hard you would probably wet yourself. She had lovely hair; in those days people were using pressing combs to straighten their hair; hair relaxer was not a thing then. After doing it for years, Ms Jane, decided it was time to stop, and she began wearing her hair natural. She told Rose and her other siblings that one night she had a dream: she saw herself in a church and there were people within the church worshiping. During this vision they told her that the hot comb wasn't good for her brain. Well, Rose's mom believed it was a message from God and so she had to obey.

Rose's mother had her own yam farm; it was much smaller in size than her husband's one, but by planting quick crops like carrots, tomatoes, and cabbage, she was able to sell it to market vendors. That's how she managed to earn herself some extra money.

Rose's land of birth was a beautiful place to live but to achieve your goals requires hard work and determination, just as in any other country. In her community the men were only farmers because they had no other choices.; some were not even good at it, but they had no other profession available to them. Some people were destitute, but were determined to survive, even giving away their children to family members who were more financially stable; that shows how hard life was. It was sad but that was their only option; Rose's aunt gave up one of her daughters to her sister, and she would go visit them sometimes. Rose and her siblings were lucky in that way, they all stayed together as a family and that was a good thing.

The farmers had different seasons throughout the year when their crops would be ready to reap; gungo peas was one such splendid crop. When it was ripe and ready, it would be picked and prepared, ready to be eaten. Rose's mom would use it to make delicious meals, rice, and peas, or gungo soup, even stews; Ms Jane was a great cook, – her food was finger licking good. Whenever Ms Jane cooked gungo pea soup, she would add freshly picked ripe corns from the fields. Rose and her sisters would make sure that the peas were thoroughly clean before they were ready for cooking.

Rose and her sisters had a game that they would play, using the corn from the food. Ship sail, it was called. Each person would be standing in a corner of the house, where they could all see each other. The game went by rotation, each person picking off the corn grain, placing it into their palm. Everyone was given a chance to guess how many corn grains there were, whoever got the correct number was the winner, and got to keep the corn. Rose enjoyed playing the game, she was cunning at it, often ending up with everyone's corn. Her sisters. Jena and Del, would be upset about losing their corn to Rose, and begging to have some back. "Please Sis," said Jena, her youngest sister, can I have some back? Rose kept laughing, pretending to have eaten it all, but eventually, after looking at Jena`s sad little face, she gave her back her portion.

Del half smiled, with the hope that she too might receive her corn back.

"Here, you just take it," Rose, would say, jokingly. "Thank you" her sister would politely reply, before running off to eat her corn. After they finished eating, Del said to the others

"let's go and play rope skipping".

"In a minute," Rose replied. "Mama asked that I wash the dishes first." Their mother came out of the house with a plate in her hands, then she said,

"tomorrow your father will be working on the farm. He'll be needing your help carrying yams from the field."

Rose replied, "OK, mom. I don't mind helping papa". Rose said to Del

"we got no say in the matter because we're children. The only issue is that steep gully we're going to climb with the loads on our heads".

She mumbled under her breath as she walked away, picking up a stone in her hand.

During this time, Verna, and Maria both already had their first child at the age of sixteen, about three years apart. It was difficult for them, having to live at home, often reminded of what a disappointment they were to their family. Verna had a son who was born at home; in those days people like them didn't really go to hospitals to have their babies. Instead, the midwives made house calls. When Verna's son was about four years old. she didn't have any choice but to go out and work, so Bob was raised by his father's side of the family. She would often return on the weekends, to visit the family with her son. Maria had fallen pregnant at the same age as Verna, three years later. He too was born at home and his name was Kevin. He grew up in the same house as Rose and the others, and he was more like a little brother, rather than being a nephew. Maria also had to work and support herself and her child, and so she too left home when Kevin, was about five years old. Like Verna she would also come home to visited on weekends. Leaving the community was a good move for them, as it helped them to find their own path. Maria never returned home to live; she was always away working. They worked as live-in domestic helpers for many years.

While Verna, was away working, six years later she came home pregnant with her second child. Well, as you can imagined her father was terribly upset about how careless and stupid she had been. Verna had nowhere else to live, and it was obviously clear that she would end up as a single mother. A couple of months later her daughter was born, who she named Kelly. Financially she was struggling to cope, and after a few years her only option was to go into full time employment. So, now Kevin and Kelly became permanent additions to the family. Verna did what she could but most of the responsibilities were left to the grandparents. It was surprisingly strange how well the grandchildren were treated by Rose's dad.

While Maria was away working, she met her long-term partner, Ricky, who later became her husband. Years later, she moved in with him and his family in the parish of Clarendon. He treated her well, and she was happy. His household consisted of his mother, father, and daughter Sharlene.

Rose and her younger sisters and her brother ,Willy, had their own tasks ahead of them regarding helping on the farm. When the harvest time came for the crops to be reaped sometimes they had to stay home from school to help on the farm. At that time Kevin was too young help. The yams would be dug from the ground using a machete by the workers. Rose and her younger siblings would gather baskets of yams on their heads, carrying them to a safe place. In most cases the yam fields were in gullies, so their job was to carry them to the top of the hill, where it was flat enough so they would not roll away. Rose's dad had a donkey, a fine beast, whose full purpose was to carry loads. Rose's dad gave the beast an unusual name; he was called Sam Basel, and he was without a doubt the strongest beast Rose had ever known.

At times Rose felt sorry for the beast. He had a sort of designed amour for his back, when carrying loads; his back was padded with thick mats that were made from a special straw. Two hampers were placed on the donkeys back, so the load could be carried to the designated location. As much as Rose's dad had many farms, he didn't have much money set aside for a rainy day. Most of the time he was too busy being drunk or lending his money to whoever had a sad story. The people

31

who borrowed his money never paid it back; occasionally he wasn't able to recall who he lent it to. Some prevaricated, life got the better of them regarding payment, and that was contrary indeed. When Rose`s dad, was not drinking alcohol he was the nicest and calmest person you could meet; that just shows how alcohol can transform an individual, when consumed to excess.

He was short, his complexion was dark as a cup of cocoa without the milk, so much the opposite of Rose`s mom. His facial expression was mostly serious but in some strange way very approachable. He had two hats, one he wore to his farm every day to work, the other was a felt hat, Yes! that was definitely his favourite. His body movements would change immediately he put his felt hat on, especially if he was dressed up. Rose and the others found him hysterical, stepping out with confidence, he was so sure of himself, as if he was floating on a cloud. He was a comedian in his own right. Rose and her sisters used to call him George, the character from the TV series 'The Jeffersons', except that Rose`s mom, was no Wheezy; she was too sacred to do anything. His temperament was of a quiet nature, and that was surprising for mostly everyone, considering the other person he became during his intoxication. He treated his children and Rose`s mom differently whenever he was sober, especially the girls. Rose and her sisters were overjoyed when he was in his calmer mood. They prayed diligently for their dad to remain sober, but that was mostly not the case. 'Maybe God, was sleeping,' Rose thought.

Maybe he did provide for his family in the best way he knew how. They had food on the table regardless as to whatever it was. For the most part Rose and the others got a secondary school education, except for Tom and Joe who only completed primary school. If you needed a higher education, working and sending yourself back to school, would be a good option. He provided for his family, in the best way he knew so that the children could survive, in the massive world ahead of them. A few of Rose's siblings were outstanding students, during the time they were attending school, others, particularly the oldest siblings, not so much. Everyone was given the chance to learn something, but whatever you did with that moment, was entirely up to you. Rose's dad had a poor educational background so learning a skill would be more difficult for him. People were also very underprivileged; he often spoke of how little his family had when they were children.

Whenever writing letters to his aunts abroad he would ask his children to help him, because he struggled to write anything except the most basic of English. He spoke Jamaican Patois, so Rose, or any other members of her siblings, would write his letters for him. Often it would be hilarious; trying to choke back the laugher was almost impossible to do, especially for Rose's mom. He had a way of changing his voice, he was like a kitten convinced of being a lion, and wasn't sure what he was trying to accomplish. After several failed attempts , and throwing away great wads of spoilt writing paper, in the end, common sense would prevail. Most of the time what he wanted them to write would be considerably difficult to understand but they normally figured it out. Rose's mom was very different; she was able to write her own letters with little or no help, even her reading ability was more advanced than his, an advantage she had over him. Rose's smile widened.

Christmas was one of the most remarkable holidays for Rose and the sisters. For Rose, it represented jollification and good will to all men; that was good enough for her. The rest of her sisters were just as excited; Jenna and Del couldn't wait to see what they would get for

Christmas. Unconventionally, they didn't really believe in Santa Claus; apparently, they had no chimney. The closest Rose and her sisters had ever got to Santa was on the television their uncle from Canada had given them. Watching films of him handing out presents to the less fortunate children or dropping them off at midnight. At some point in their solitary mind, they might have believed that he was real, but after years, of watching and waiting there was still no sign of him or his reindeers anywhere. Every year Rose's mother would take one of the children with her to do the Christmas shopping That year it was Rose's turn.

"So, Rose," Del asked, "Are you glad about going with mama?"

" Yep," she remarked happily, "but I honestly wish mama could let you come". "Yeah. Me too, Rose! As you already know, mama can only afford to take only one of us with her". "I know," she agreed. Del knew that next year would be her turn and so she waited.

Grand market night was the highlight for many children, but not for Rose. She went through her seventeen years of living at home without having any memory of having been to one. Maybe her parents thought that she was too young, or who knows what they might believe? Rose tossed and turned in bed the night before she went Christmas shopping with her mother. She even dreamt that her mother left her behind. Poor Rose woke up in a sweat, frightened out of her body, she could almost feel her heart popping out her chest. As she looked around, it was clear that night lingered on, in all its presence. 'My goodness, thank god, it's only a dream' she thought to herself, or more like a nightmare, she sighed! The rest of the night Rose hadn't closed her eyes, she couldn't afford to be left behind. It was now morning; you could feel the passion of Christmas; it was a big deal for everyone. She

34

quickly got out of bed, ran to the door of her mother's room, calling out her name. "Mama, what time are we leaving?"

They would be doing the shopping at a nice little town called Christiana, where vendors and shoppers alike were purchasing for the holidays.

"Soon Rose," her mother shouted back to her.

"Oh my, I can`t wait to see the town lights," she said to Jena and Del. It was the only place she would see a few Christmas lights, and fancy decorations. Music was playing loudly, with everyone conducting their business, sellers and buyers alike.

Rose and her mother were now ready to go; as they left, Jenna and Del stood on the veranda watching. Rose was smiling from cheek to cheek. They had to walk a good while before catching the bus. When Rose and her mother finally arrived at the bus stop a few people were already there waiting. "Good morning," her mother greeted them; it was a case of everyone knew each other in some way or another. After a while the old blue bus arrived; on top of it were piled the baskets of goods and vegetables of the vendors who were going to the market. Rose's mother held her hand, pulling her closer, to step forward; the conductor was shouting, "move over a little, miss" to one woman. The ride into town wasn't a cosy one, as Rose had to stand all the way for such a long time. People were bracing on you, so close in your space. Rose, hated that. Her mother had managed to get a seat; it was the principle of giving the elderly folks first choice. The bus picked up almost everyone. 'Jesus ,what a greedy driver. Next he`ll be packing passenger on top of the bus,' Rose thought. The passengers were now grumbling, considering the bus was feeling humid.

Eventually, the bus was at its destination, Rose was excited to see the town in all its elements, Christmas music was playing everywhere as she had anticipated. Christmas lights, everything seemed so perfect, the carol singing sounded so heavenly. The Christmas Eves that she saw on television were more magical, because they had snowman and elves, but who was complaining? . "Come on Rose," her mother said, as they walked toward the marketplace. Rose was amazed at all the lovely things that she saw. There were fake Santas hanging in shop windows, dressed in their finest. Her mother stopped at a vendor's stall, where she brought callaloo and roasted breadfruit. She picked up other items that they didn't cultivate themselves. Rose's mother then went to a few stores, buying shoes and dresses for Del and Jenna; there was one of each for Rose, too. Her face lit up so brightly, you would think she was wearing the sun. Rose's mother had now completed their shopping for the day, but before they went to the bus station she had one more place to stop and that was the bakery to buy fresh bread and juicy beef patties.

Rose felt hungry and exhausted from the busy day she'd had. Her mother gave her one of the patties and a small bottle of Bigga, which was the most popular drink then. "We should eat before getting the bus, Rose," mother insisted.

"OK, mama," she replied. The bus station wasn't far away, so getting there was easy. Rose carried two shopping bags in her hands. They mounted the bus; it was occupied by only a few passengers at present. This time Rose was able to sit with her mother, placing her head against the back of the seat. When they got home her sisters, Jenna and Del, were exhilarated to see them. They rushed out to meet them; you'd think they'd been gone for years.

"Rose," they both spoke at once, as she looked back at them happily.

"Did you saw what mama brought us?"

Yeah," you`ll both be the gladdest ever," she reassures them. Rose was right They were overjoyed to receive such lovely pairs of shoes and dresses. 'Tomorrow is Christmas day, and I can`t wait to wear my new clothes,' Del thought to herself with a smile.

"Anything happening up the street, Rose?" Jenna asked with much expectancy. "Yes There`s men working on the merry- go-round, pool box, and a couple of other entertainments. "Oh, isn't it splendid," she called as she ran off to play. Christmas was filled with every activity as that was like a dream come true for a child. It was amazing, how everyone seemed cheerful and happy celebrating the festive season. Many children from all around came to join in the fun and excitement.

"Oh, how I wish everyday was Christmas." Listening to carols was adequate reason for her. She lay her dress out on the bed. Apart from going to church, holidays were the only time they got new clothes.

"Jenna and Del, I'll be leaving soon."

Rose told them their own dresses would appear equally exciting, nothing could stop them now. Then Rose and her sisters were dressed up, looking quite sophisticated – well, at least that's how they felt, wearing their brand-new outfits and ribbons in their hair. Rose's oldest sister, Verna, was the specialist when it came to baking Christmas cake. She designed the oven from a metal pan, using coals as the fireplace. Rose's mother would be cooking the Christmas dinner, and all the different smells were divine. It wasn't perfect but they loved it, and were happy and content even if it was just for a day. After Christmas was over, things went back to normal, like it never was in existence; such a pity, Rose thought.

Rose and the younger sisters and brother Willy were always together, as far as she could remember. The oldest brothers were doing their own thing, and never went to school during the time that Rose was attending. Maria and Verna the oldest sisters were already mothers; having had their first child each, their days of schooling were over. The only work that was acquirable for them during that time was being a domestic help; it was crucial having that independence and maintaining their own needs. Rose's father wasn't going be responsible for them.

Chapter 3
THE BEGINING OF
THE DARK DAYS

Tom was the oldest son; he appeared to be quiet and most of the time seemed unhappy and lost; he had an unmotivated approach towards work. Rose believed that was due to his lack of interest; he sealed his faith in a negative way. Even on a good day his mood would always remain the same. The atmosphere between him and his dad was of a hostile nature, and often felt like an omen of things to come. At the age of sixteen Tom, was thrown out from the house he called home, and the place he shared with his siblings. Being the oldest didn't work much in his favour, having to leave home at that age. His chance of having a successful life was now hopeless and that was proven many years later. Rose's father believed that her brother was unscrupulous, something that he was totally against. It was the ultimate unforgiveable act, and whosoever committed such an offence had no chance of staying in his house. As a young boy of such a tender age one cannot begin to imagine the turmoil that went through his mind. They saw him occasionally due to the fact he was living with families who lived nearby. Even though Tom wasn't living at the family home anymore life wasn't any easier for him. He was free but continued to struggle with his life. Tom only had a primary school education, and that ended in the ninth grade. It wasn't clear, why Tom didn't receive a secondary education, one can only make a guess. That wasn't a lot to go on with, considering his age. And by the way, who was going to hire an underage boy? He sure had to grow up fast; he had to learn survival. He ended up making some bad choices that still reflected on his life for many years after. For the most part Rose believed he could've been redeemed if he'd fought harder; if he really wanted to. His attitude towards work had been reformed; he was basically on his own and his alternatives were limited. Sadly, as an adult Tom, developed the same genetics as his dad, in some areas even worse, abusing his women and being constantly drunk.

- Willy too had his full share of beatings; he was even tied up and beaten until he wet himself, and that memory still sits quite vividly in Rose's mind. His judgement unfolded and was cast upon him, when his father sent him to purchase meat from a shop in the area. It wasn't clear what happened to the money but he reported back that it got lost. Being confused about his dilemma, sadly he thought by still going to the shop and ordering the meat, that was somehow a good idea. Looking back then, he knew that it wouldn't be an honourable choice. However, he brought the meat home, but not by himself or the way you would think. The shop owner took the time from his busy schedule to drive him home. Everyone was terrified for him; the expression on his face – Oh, it hurt Rose every time she recalled it. There were other men in the van, and they claimed he took the meat off the counter without paying for it. His dad was filled with rage, professing that Willy had ruined his good name. He endeavoured to explain, but that fell on deaf ears; all his dad wanted to do was to punish him in the worst way possible, and so he did. He was sober as he hadn't had a drink that day, the look that was in Willy's eyes was pure surrender; there wasn't anything else he could say or do that wouldn't intensify the situation. Rose and her sisters were weeping for their brother, watching, as their father tortured him savagely. All Rose felt for him was sorrow, and emptiness; she saw someone that day that she didn't recognise, and that was petrifying. Rose`s mother was afraid of her dad; she had no courage or confidence at the time. She never condoned what he did to Willy. A part of Rose believed she wanted to help but didn't know how because she, too, had her full share of trouble.

Rose's mother was also a Jamal school teacher; it was a programme to assist individuals who were illiterate. It was an honourable thing that she did considering the pay. She kept it on the veranda of the house. She would place some chairs there, making sure that her pupils were comfortable. She tried her best so that it would appear as a regular classroom even though it was Rose`s family home. It was surprisingly odd, seeing young people that should have being at school, or at least having some educational background. It was evident they were unable to even sign their names, but were now attending night classes. It goes to show how unfortunate some people were, even attending school was deemed impossible for their parents.

Rose and her siblings were not allowed to be present during these classes. Ms Jane thought it was better for her students, some of whom were embarrassed to be seen in such position. She often encouraged her husband to attend but he was a proud man. One evening before class began, Rose's mom said to her husband, "it would be good if you could attend".

She had an uncertain expression on her face, as if she already knew what he would say. As she stood in the hallway looking at him, waiting for an answer.

"Who me? you must be joking," he replied. He had too much pride to been sitting with the others. They thought highly of him, because most of them worked on his farm and he must have thought that it would lessen his character; he wouldn't be caught dead among them. Well just as she expected his answer would be. He looked at her as if he were possessed, but she did not respond, just walked away, and went outside. He continued to speak, but no one was listening, his behaviour was surprising, you would be forgiven for thinking she had done something really horrible. Rose shook her head feeling annoyed. She went after her mother and said,

"mama, are you OK? Don't worry. That is his loss. It would help him to develop". "Things will get better, one day. You already know what he's like". Her mom, looked at Rose and smiled, but she could see that she was hurting. "It´s ok Rose. I'm used to his behaviour, my child, I'm alright." As a child it was best to stay out of grown-up business, and so she kept quiet.

During his intoxication transformation Rose's mom would suffer the most abuse, sometimes physically, but more often it would be verbally. He was like a roaring lion, firing at anyone in his path, thirsty for blood. Everyone in the household was always panicking. Whenever the crops were ripe enough to reap, that was when he would squander his money, spending it on alcohol as if toiling in the fields was a game. He made it look easy; just smelling the rum glass would transform him into this horrid person that didn't care about anyone, except for being a tormenter to his family. All the minor little irrelevant things that they thought were water under the bridge, now it would be a good time to be worried, because he would remember it like it was yesterday. Considering the outcome would only be more than you'd bargained for, wishing the night would never come. How ironic, it was always convenient for him not to remember the horrible things that he did or said. Rose thought that he was pretending; he probably thought he was as clever as an owl, and was more in denial than she believed. How could he not realise what he'd done? Is that even possible? Surely, if he was wide awake how could he not know. Perhaps the shame was too much for him to bear. Rose wished that so dearly, but to be honest, she was rationalising his behaviour to make sense of it all. They all would suffer in different ways; it was not a walk in the park for anyone. Rose's younger siblings were aware of what was happening; besides, they were only two and three years apart.

Willy was different compared to Rose's other older brothers; he worked hard on the farm with his dad. After a while he was able to cultivate his own, and he was pleased with himself. He became more independent regarding his own future and his vision. He was headstrong and knew what he wanted.

Rose and Willy were awfully close; they shared many secrets and looked out for each other. They often, talked about how they would help each other when they got older, whoever would progress first or leave home. When Willy met Wendy, he was about twenty one years old. She became a big part of his life. Years later she became his wife and the mother of his two adorable sons. Wendy and everyone got on well, she was easy to speak with, a lovely girl. It felt as if they knew her years before they met her.

John was Rose's dad's name; Papa John, the children would sometimes call him, or just papa. A couple of years later things were getting better as the prices of yam sales were hitting the roof and for the longest time his finance changed immensely for the better. He decided that he would invest into having a business, putting some of his money to use. He eventually built a grocery shop, and built additional rooms, one for each of his daughters. He did attempt to change his life, but the alcohol always got the better of him. One of his theories was an honourable one, that when his daughters moved out, if life were unkind to them, they would have a home to return to, but regrettably, for most that was not the case at all.

As time went by Willy, felt it was time to move out the family house. No one could blame him. Living in that house was overly exhausting and as a young man he needed his privacy. He moved into one of the rooms that was built onto the grocery shop. He lived there for four years, while building his own home.

It was the summer of 1988, a year when it seemed that the weather was all sunshine and rain, fresh air, everything always looking vibrant and green, even if elsewhere it was all gloom and doom. Occasionally Jamaica would experience some hurricanes, earthquakes, and other natural disasters. The building was completed, and the business was flourishing. Everything seemed great to Rose, and her siblings. They thought it would be the era of prosperity and success for their family. For the most part it was ok, until the next inevitable disaster. He was excited about having his own business, he did a good job making sure that the business was promoted, well stocked with every food product there was. It was supported by most of the residents in the community although there were a few who weren't too enthusiastic about the idea. The trouble began when Papa John started stocking alcohol in his store. Now instead of having to buy it elsewhere he had a ready supply constantly at hand. After he started to consume his profits, things went from bad to worse.

His old drinking buddies were now popping up out of the woodwork, as if it was an apocalypse. Playing devil's advocate, no way out, and who is going to help them now. Rose sat on the veranda, and as usual, searching for answers by questioning herself, like she was the only person in the world. Her only thought was that God most have abandoned them. Why was he still allowing this to happened? Have they not been through enough? His behaviour was worsening; he would be in the bar till the late hours of the night, with his rum buddies brawling and shouting, with no regards for anyone.

After much evaluation, his business became his closest friend, so he decided that moving out of the house, and into one of the rooms that were built on his place of business was more satisfying for him in order to rule his kingdom. It was a relief for everyone, not having to endure his malicious behaviour, and disturbing Ms Jane, and the children. At least now when he was intoxicated and misbehaving, Ms Jane would be safe from his abuse, even though it did not stop him from trying. He would still come into the house whenever he was hammered, always picking on someone and causing problems. One night he came into the house as usual, as high as a kite. Rose and the others believed he pretended to be under the influence to reveal his hidden emotion, and then carried out his attack.

As he went into their bedroom, he began shouting and cussing, and a few minutes later Rose's mother was yelling out for help. Rose and her two sisters, Jenna and Del ran to the door screaming, murder as loud as they could, hoping he would fear the noise and stop hurting their mom. He came storming out the room, stood at the door like some old dragon, puffing out fire. "What`s all the noises for?", he demanded and then continued his swearing as usual. Before he could say another word , Rose, and her sisters dashed through the main door and out into the dark of the night. The worst part was that most of their older siblings had already moved out. Verna, the oldest sister, was still living at home but feared even her own shadow. Willy was the only one who had enough the courage to do anything but unfortunately he wasn't at home, so they had to go and find him.

It was dark outside but that couldn't slow them down, running as if the devil were chasing them. Finally, they got to Aunt Clare's shop ten minutes away from home. At one point they had to stop for Jenna, who was feeling fatigued from running. Rose held her hand walking alongside her. Del was a few paces ahead the first time that happened, and by the time Rose and her sister got there he was already coming. "Willy," Jenna shouted, "come quickly, papa is killing mama," she said looking distraught. She was the youngest, God knew how horrifying that must have felt, tears running down her face. Rose was broken-hearted. Del, had a heart condition; Rose, was worried about her health too, being the oldest of the three sisters and all. Her job was to make sure they were ok. She tried her best, but it wasn't an easy responsibility.

They were crying because in their mind, their mother was probably dead. Willy was older than Rose, but he was frightened and angry all at the same time. "How dare he? That man needs to be stopped. God

knows I'm fed up with him. Why does he think he has the right?"
Willy started running but Rose kept back with the others. They didn't
seem to care much about the dark; being there felt better than going
back into that house. When they got home, Rose's dad was in the
bedroom. By this time the sound of silence was haunting the house.
Willy shouted, "Are you ok," and at first, mama didn't answer. "Oh
my god, she is dead"? they probably thought. You could tell by the
unsettling looks, and their faces, gazing at each other. Willy saw his
sisters faces; his only reaction was calling out a second time. Their
mother came out of the room looking terrified and shaken.

The building was built in the yard, so at times you were able to hear
whatever was happening next door. Sometimes it would be shameful,
hearing from passers- by what took place in the following days. He
would give away goods from the business, and not knowing where the
profit of the night went; half the time he was unable to remember
what he did and to whom. A few episodes occurred, while he was not
in his right mind, or maybe he was; that's a mystery, what with him
hurting one of his drinking buddies by smashing one of his hand really
badly. It did not go down well; his buddy stopped speaking to him for
a long time. Everyone was gossiping about it, and eventually it became
a closed topic. Some people believed that he was probably bewitched;
he would not indulge or consider such nonsense. For a man that had
so much faith, a strong believer in god, it was difficult to comprehend
his actions, especially his children.

In the same year of 1988, there was a terrible hurricane, called
Gilbert, that hit the island; it was a catastrophe for many families.
Before the hurricane hit all the signs were visible to see. Rose and her
siblings had never experienced such weather before. However, they were

excited about having a hurricane, not knowing the damage and impact it would cause. Her older siblings were terrified; Verna was crying like the world was coming to an end. It was amusing for Rose and her younger siblings, and so they laughed at her, but not in a mean way. First came the rain, and then the wind, it was moving in at maximum speed. No-one was laughing now; instead, they were as frightened as mice. Rose`s dad and some of their neighbours barricaded the windows, securing everything as best they could, but even that was not enough to prevent the damage that was to come.

The roof top of Rose`s house had now had its marching orders, and was already lifting from its base from every corner. The men quickly got ladders and were climbing through the hurricane, to save their place of rest. Everyone was affected; Rose and her family saved twenty-five families within their building during the hurricane disaster. Their homes were damaged, roof tops were blown off houses, debris everywhere. Even though the building was not yet completed, it was secure. The top of the building was made from decking method, and Rose's dad intended that in the future he would continue building additional rooms on top. For the longest while Rose's dad wasn't intoxicated; he was human after all. It was a delightful time; everyone seemed so unified, and they could be a normal family for once fulfilling Rose's hopes and dreams for as long as she could remember. Under the circumstances, there was peace at last. Rose smiled to herself as she kept watching the rain pouring down. In spite of his imprudent behaviour, some people did genuinely like him; he had a kind heart, and a caring approach towards his fellow neighbours in need.

When the hurricane was over, everyone went back to their homes, to salvage what little they could. It was a really hard time, Rose's family home was flooded throughout with water, most of what was in their house was damaged. The ceiling of the house fell through, due to the pressure of water that had settle on the roof. Rose's dad had to enforce holes into the celling, pushing the water out. Well, it was a tragedy; some families were hit harder than others but regardless, they had all suffered. Everyone was given assistance from the local Parish Counsellor except for Rose`s family. Ms Jane, did ask for a few zinc sheets to help with the fixing of the roof but she was ignored. They didn't give Rose's mother a reason why. However, the persons who were responsible didn't like Rose's dad much. How sad it was. You could tell by observing; looking hard and long enough it was clear Rose saw, that her parents felt abandon by the community, even though they were putting on a brave face. As a young girl in that place and time, you saw things that probably you should not have, but were not allowed to ask questions.

It was the worst hurricane Rose, and her family have ever seen or experienced. Her mother reminisced about one she had experienced many years before. Looking in the distance, she paused breathing deeply and said, "a few people I knew passed away then". It took a long-time fixing and getting things back to normality, considering they did everything without any assistance from their local PM. People seemed to assume that Rose's dad was financial stable, and no-one ever seemed to be concerned about how they got by. Except of course, whenever he was intoxicated people would be gossiping and looking at them, as if they were from a different planet.

The shops in the community had a limited amount of food suppling the area after Hurricane Gilbert, and everything was expensive. The farmers had no food; most of their crops were ruined including Rose`s dad. But even though he had a limited crop remaining, he was still able to share with his fellow neighbours. Even through his previous betrayal, he just carried on as normal, still doing what he did best, and that was sharing. When he was intoxicated he would show more compassion towards them than his own family, as it was easier to see them as his enemy. Rose felt nothing but anger towards him. She knew it wasn't right. "How dare he?" she kept saying to herself.

Whenever Rose's dad wasn't hammered, he was surprisingly humble and kept to himself. He liked his own space, and anyone could have a regular conversation with him. It was terrible confusing most of the time, like he had this split personality. Rose, often wondered if something might have happened to him. Was it possible that one of his own parents was cruel and mean to him, as he was to his own when he was intoxicated? They didn't really know, although they had heard strange stories about his upbringing; some were not great. The children didn't know either of their grandfathers, they, unfortunately, having both died before the younger siblings were born. After Tom had left home, Rose's mother took it hard. There is an old saying that goes, 'you are the product of your environment and if one does not thrive for empowerment, you will always be a victim of your surroundings'.

Rose's mom was the subject of accusation for everything, above anything else, even when she knew nothing about the matter. She was not exempt from the harsh and brutal words of Rose`s dad, and occasionally it came with the physical, too. As the years passed, things remained the same, the fear deepened, especially when he got drunk and that became a regular thing. Whenever he went out, they would expect him to return dead drunk. Even though he wasn't staying in the house, it didn't mean anything. The fact that he built it gave him every power. It wasn't a custom to go out carrying house keys.

There was always someone home to open the door. When at nights he knocked on the door, someone had better respond. Anticipating the worst was everyone's problem, Rose would often hope that he would not come home. He was like an elephant coming, breaking through the tranquillity of the night where you couldn't hear a pin if one fell a hundred miles away. He would be shouting the odds, swearing, and probably fighting with his own shadow in the brightness of the moonlight, thinking that he was being followed. The moon beams were looking enchanting, shining from the skies, breaking through every dark corner, leaving nowhere to hide. They would hear him banging the door, and shouting for someone to let him in his house, the house, he kept reminding them, that he built from nothing. If no one was willing to open the house door, he would continue with his threats, saying that he would take an axe and break the door down. They would often visualise him as the wolf, in the three little pigs' tale; that was how they characterized him, how scary that must have been. Well, hell would break loose when he was finally inside; no one would be sleeping that night, especially Rose's poor mother.

It was a cycle that would repeat itself as they got older and their relationships deteriorated, history almost repeating in the same order. After Tom was gone Rose's other brothers were in line. Joe used to help on the farm and his father would pay him for his service, although ideally, he wasn't allowed to do whatever he wanted to do on the farm. But things took a sour turn, leaving them bitter towards each other. Rose's father had a policy; what was his belonged to him only, once you defiled that, you became an enemy, beyond the state line. There wasn't much, anyone could do, just watch the chips as they fell. Rose was unable to figure out what could have caused such hostility between a father and son; it was a mystery to her. As luck would have it, there was a farming program designed to give young men an opportunity. Rose's mother knew the lady who was managing the programme and so he got an opportunity to change his life. He went to America, working on fruit orchards, picking apples. After six months the programme came to an end, leaving him no choice but to return home. Since Joe went away on the farm work programme, that gave him some leverage for freedom. His dad was more convinced of Joe being a failure, and was constantly ridiculing him. He continued to live at home for a while, until he finally left on his own; his capability for survival was different from Tom`s. Even though he came back home a few times after his shortcomings, there were others, who went back on the programme which continued for years. They stayed until they were able to build their own homes. Some were able to help their families, but not Joe. He got in a fight with some guy when he went on the programme and the bosses were not in favour of such behaviour, so brought his employment to an end. The company never requested him again, and they could see how disappointed he was. He was never outstanding when it came to yam farming but was good with cultivating other crops: sweet peppers, Irish potatoes, scotch bonnet pepper, and more. He used to go to the market to sell his produce.

"Good for him mama," used to say.

During the years of mistreatment that Rose's mom endured, the sleepless nights, running off to neighbours and family houses in the middle of the night was overwhelming. It was too much to endure both mentally and physically and so she suffered a mental breakdown. Life was not the same for a long time. Ms Jane had to stay with her family for a while, and with the support and love that she received she got better, but never was really the same afterwards. After a couple of weeks Ms Jane was well enough, and so she returned to the house of terror.

She learned how to manage and cope with the breakdown, but in her own time. The side effects left her with severe jitters to her body and headaches that would get the better of her. In those days mental health was a taboo, referred to as being a mad person or a lunatic. Rose's mom was fortunate in some ways considering that a lot of people did not know of this; her illness was described as having a breakdown. When Rose's mother explained her experience from her terrible ordeal, it was heart-breaking to hear, or even understand. The suffering that she went through was inconsolable to the human heart. She felt afraid, lost, and confused even hallucinating at one point. She was talking to and seeing dead people; it was not ideal to be talking about the dead, imagine seeing them! For another person to treat someone like Ms Jane was treated by the husband who he was meant to care for, its unbelievably wrong in every form.

This is not overstated; for her to be trapped away in her own mind, watching her mother as she faded away that was difficult for Rose and the others to see in that way. The youngest, couldn't remember much; didn't really understand, but they knew something was wrong. As the years went by the physical abuse grew less, but verbal abuse was more. Rose knew that it did not make much difference, those words still cut your soul as if you were hit with a stone. At the age of seventeen Rose, ran away from home. Can you imagine what lead up to that moment for her to make such a decision. It was due to the verbal abuse that she endured, and she had had enough.

It was during the summer time in 1987, the sun was beaming through the sky, you could smell the air as if the earth has been scorched. Every natural fragrance of different plants was wrapped up in one accord combined. Even though it was such a dynamic summer day, it was not going to be a glorious one for Rose. Her father must have thought that using, aggressive and unpleasant words to a child, would be the right thing to do. After years of doing that, it became a natural thing for him. Looking back on it all Rose felt disheartened. As the maltreatment intensified towards her, on the day the event took place, Rose's dad demanded she go and fetch wood from the fields. It was used in the fireplace for the cooking of meals. Those days hot plates and gas or electric cookers were not a prominent thing; you would have to be living within gated communities. She went willingly to fetch the firewood as she was told but Rose was in tears; deep in her heart she knew that the day was not going to end well.

It took her thirty minutes to complete her task, but when she returned with the bundle of wood on her head her dad was in the yard looking cross and miserable, sweating and with a deranged look in his eyes. He was holding his machete in one hand, and Rose didn't know what to think. Her heart was pounding in her chest, gasping to catch a breath as she prayed to God for his intervention upon her. As Rose removed the bundle of wood from her head, placing it upon the ground, her dad was circling like an eagle about to attack its prey. Then he struck, kicking Rose on the leg. He lifted the machete over her as if he was going to chop her into pieces She screamed out in agony but managed to run away. By then he was swearing and cursing at her like he wasn't satisfied, but she didn't stop to listen to the man. Rose's mom heard the nose and came outside from the house but never said a word, just stood there looking mortified and confused. Rose understood that it was probably better that way. What happened within the next hour was inevitable. Her mom went into the kitchen, then started to prepare lunch, probably blocking her mind from the commotion. The kitchen was built separate from the house; those day everyone had their kitchen designed in same the way. The smoke from the kitchen, would be escaping through the tiny window and making its way into the air, dancing to freedom.

Rose knew there would be no peace for her under his regime in that house; nothing but total torment was all she could expect and a constant reminder of how she was trespassing. Her mother wasn't bold enough to stand up for her children; she would just stand there without saying a word, watching as the skin was being beaten off your body.. She didn't like beating but, throwing things in your direction, hitting you anywhere on your body; if it was something she considered you deserved a whipping for, be afraid. She had a habit of waiting until Rose's dad came home, pulling him to one side to make her report, instigating what would follow. This time she had nothing to do with his deeds, but not doing anything to stop him was really hard coping with. Rose felt guilty. She couldn't bear having anyone else suffer because of her; how excruciating that would`ve been. She felt angry towards her mother, who took no action to save them from the horrible beatings. Then again maybe she couldn't have done anything. Either way there was no winning. Willy had his own issues with him, and didn't want him to make it more horrendous. Rose felt she was in a time hole and on her own with no one to turn to. With time slipping away, Rose's decision must come sooner rather than later. Thankfully her siters weren't home; if they had been the conclusion might have been different. Rose contemplated on the situation, 'Mama's in the kitchen, and will be there for a while. My father is at the farm working. That`ll give me adequate time to leave.' It was the most disheartening day of her seventeen years. It was with regret that she had to say goodbye to the home she had lived in all her life. Maybe she thought that one day she would return like the prodigal daughter? Who knows what went through her mind that day? Finally, Rose grasped that things would never change and that it would always be like this between them. And that's when her mind switched on, to take the action to leave.

Rose continued to cry with no one to comfort her. She looked down at her left thigh; it had an enormous black and blue blood clot that had settled under her skin, due to impact from the kick she had received earlier that day. Her younger siblings were not home as they were attending school. Her mother was still in the kitchen cooking, saying something to Rose, but she wasn't paying much attention. All she knew was that she had to leave, and it did not matter at what cost. She looked around to see if her dad was anywhere to be seen. Once she realised that the coast was clear, she made her decision to escape. Rose went inside the house to get her clothing. There was an old suitcase that they kept under the bed. She pulled it out and started packing, with what little clothing that she had. It was not much, because most of what she had were church clothes. It wasn't honourable taking her sisters stuff either, considering they too were short in that department. She felt nervous, her lungs hyperventilating with the fear of being caught. Her thoughts were in overdrive, thinking of the worse that could go wrong. If someone entered the house and caught her leaving what would they say, or what if her dad saw? What would he do?

Chapter 4
The JOURNEY TO CLARENDON

Rose decided, there was no way she was going to stay in that house. Clarendon was many miles away from home but that was the place she intended to go. She had no money of her own but that couldn't stop her from getting there. Even if she had to walk to the ends of the earth, it wouldn't matter to her. She snuck out of the house, pulling the old worn out suitcase behind her. Rose was scared, hands shaking and sweat running down from her face, as if she were under a waterfall. The only thought that was going through her mind was that no one should see her. What she was wearing, wasn't even comfortable enough for travelling. Most of what she had were church clothing: no sneakers, no jeans, only skirts and dresses that she would wear for church. Rose's dad had a sister that lived further up the street from their home, they had always seemed to get on well. Rose was now on the main street, giving every indication of being afraid. It was unlikely that anyone would be following behind her, especially her dad. There were a few people, around but no one seemed to notice anything. Some perhaps were wondering, why she was dressed in a long skirt and heels, pulling a suitcase behind her. Rose thoughts were now frantic; she knew that people would be whispering, asking questions; obviously, she wasn't going to the airport. Rose walked slowly towards her aunts' house.

From off the street she went down a few steps towards the house. Her aunt also had a grocery store in the same yard.

A man stood at the top of the street, and couldn't seem to stop watching her. It was odd how he was looking all the time, making it obvious what he was doing. He knew Rose, so he came closer towards her. "Nosy man!" She pretended not to see him coming, then started walking away swiftly. "Rose," he called out her name, "hold up. May I have a word.

"I'm in a hurry", she replied, "I can't stop now" but he kept following behind her leaving her no choice. Rose stopped briefly." What is it you want?

Are you alright?" he asked, his voice sounding full of concern. Looking at her he could tell that she had been crying. "Where`re you going? Did something happen?

" Sorry I've got to go, now." He then realises that something was dreadfully wrong with her. She gradually walked away, holding her head down, as she kept glazing to the floor, praying that he would just leave her alone. Rose felt embarrassed but wasn't going to start worrying about what people's opinions were. She'd had enough drama on her own plate. Her aunt was standing in her yard, attentive to what was happening.

"Hello aunty," Rose greeted her in a frail voice,.
"Come sit here, "she ushered her to a chair, that was on her veranda. "Now tell me," she said eagerly, "what`s wrong with you"? Rose explained as much as she could, her aunt was beyond herself being upset. "What happened to you Rose", she said persistently. She told her aunt as to what took place, and how her father kicked her and tried to attack her with his machete. Rose, aunt was really upset

about her brother's behaviour. "So where are you going now?" she asked looking agitated. Rose looked vaguely at her, then replied that she was going to Maria`s, to her sister who was living in Clarendon.

"Aunty I've no money," Rose told her, as the tears kept rolling down her face but I`m not, going to return home." Her voice was filled with determination. I would rather walk all day, if I must, than go back to that house. Your brother is a terrible man," Rose said, sounding exhausted. Aunt Clare reach for her purse and gave Rose, thirty dollars for her journey. "

Take this she said, it will take you to Clarendon and there`s a little extra. Please be safe," her aunt repeated, looking deeply concern.

Well, you would probably think that Rose's aunt, would have encouraged her to go back home, but that wasn't the case. Instead, she told her to hurry up and get to the bus stop, before someone realised that she was missing, and that was what she did. She believed deep down that Aunt Clare, knew that her brother had a nasty temper, even though she loved him dearly. When it came to his siblings, he would walk through fire for them. That was great, and shows that he was only human after all, and was kind and loyal to them, too. In those days mobile phones were not a popular thing, so Rose had no source of communication to call anyone. She felt so alone, confused and empty with more questions than answer overflowing in her mind. She walked close to the bushes; in case anyone was following behind her. Her first thought was to hide in them. But luckily for her no one did come after her. Rose got to the bus stop and waited for the bus. It felt like forever even though, it arrived after only about ten minutes. As she entered the bus, Rose saw a woman that she knew, but she held her head down to the floor, avoiding eye contact with everyone. The journey was uncomfortably; inside the bus it was hot and crowded, and some of the passenger had newspaper fanning themselves, desperate to get a breath of fresh air.

The bus, left no passengers behind, so everyone crowed on board and there was very little space for them. Rose felt suffocated; all her frustration pent up inside and this was making it worse. Nevertheless, the bus kept on accruing more and more passengers ,until they arrived at the town central, where most of the people got off assuming it was their destination. There were vendors throughout the street selling, whatever they could get their hands on, even children that should be in school. "Bag juice" shouted a boy dressed in raggedy clothes

"Miss," as he directed his attention towards Rose, but she had no interest in what he was selling, or even saying. He stood there observing her. "Miss" he continued, this time she held up her head up slowly, eyeballing his present. "Sorry to bother you, miss" but could you please buy one of my juices?" She was astonished at how young he looked. he should`ve been in school, she thought.

"Fifty cents for one miss!" he said, licking his dry lips together. "I haven't eaten since morning. I just need buy a Patti."

Rose felt sad for the boy." Here`s a dollar. Sell me one of your juices, then." "Oh, thank you miss," he said as he handed her the juice, He then dipped into a teeny-weensy coin bag, around his waist. "Here your change."

Rose, managed to smile at him. Deep down she felt sorry for him. "It`s OK, keep it."

The boy's eyes were filled with gratitude. "Thank you miss, Safe journeys," he said as he walked away, hastily.

Rose had been wondering about the boy. How unfortunate it must be for him, hustling to survive when he should be in school. How horrible! Some people's circumstances are so difficult, even breathing seems unbearable. For a moment she was lost, thinking about what his life might be like. It was time for the bus to leave the station.

" Two more can hold," the conductor shouted, staring through the crowd with eyes, like a predator. They often prefer to have a full bus load before moving, but that day wasn't going to be the one. Rose was feeling fatigued given the day she'd had. She changed her position. 'Moving closer to an open window seat. would be ideal for the rest of my journey' she thought to herself. Off the bus went again. The driver was playing some gospel music; the one that grabbed Rose's attention was 'Jesus is the answer for all your questions', the singer kept repeating. She felt overwhelmed, but kept her composure," I won't cry" she told herself. The bus came to another town where Rose needed to get out so she could catch a second bus. "Final stop" the conductor reminded the passengers.

Rose took her suitcase from the bus, and hauled it along beside her, looking around to see the other bus she needed to board. A man came towards her shouting, "Miss, where are you going"? Rose eyeballed him with curiosity,

" I mean, your destination,".

"Oh, I'm going to May Pen she finally answered him. She had certainly not travelled that far on her own before, even though, several years before this all happened she had stayed with her sister for a short period. The man took her luggage and process ed towards a white minibus; its exterior seemed old and tired, like it had been driven through much hard weather. Rose sat in the bus This time she chose to sit in the middle, there were a lot of stories about how fast the drivers would drive, to do as many trips as possible, to make as much money as they could. "Ready, driver", the conductor yelled out as he seated himself close to the door. Rose wished she were going at her sister, under happier circumstances. The heat of the sun was becoming more intensified, and people on the bus were perspiring uncontrollably. She was almost at her stop; she could see the farms with their animals and people selling fruit, the thing that stood out most for her, was the gas station at the crossroad. "One stop, driver" Rose shouted, feeling distressed. She got off the bus, crossing the main road, to get to the other side; her doubts and fear were starting to emerge, flowing like a volcano. The road was long, filled with potholes, and with cane fields on both side of the street; she could smell the air being polluted with animal odours, especially the chicken coops.

She remembered that transportation, was not at its best, in this area and walking was a more reliable choice, so Rose kept moving faster despite everything. It took her awhile before she saw anyone, thank god she thought to herself, was beginning to feel scared of her own shadow trailing behind her. Everything in that place, was twice its normal size; the mosquitos were like gigantic wasps from the 'Land of Giants' film.

"Rose," someone called out her name. it was coming from a crowd she passed by, 'I'll just turn around and smile. That should be enough. I don't have time to stop', she thought to herself so that's what she did. Rose was almost at her sister's house, but the place looked different, some improvements had been done to it. Another woman came out of her yard, and stood at the side of the road, looking inquisitively at Rose. But Rose held her head, and passed her as if she wasn't there; old habits die hard. 'I remember you. Always up into other people's affairs.

Finally, Rose was standing at the gate, the yard in its fruit-bearing abundance, and she was looking to see if there was anyone in sight. It was almost evening, which was a relief for her, as she finally reached her journey. Maria, Rose`s sister, was very surprised to see her, of course, and no one expected to be there. Maria was sitting on the edge of her bed reading a book. The front door to her bedroom was open due to the heat of the day. When Rose arrived at her sister's house, she began shouting her name. "Maria", are you here?" as she kept walking towards the veranda. There were three mongrel dogs in the yard, barking and wagging their tail, moving towards Rose who was not impressed nor happy to see them. She looked down to see how near they were, her experience with dogs didn't sit well. It's not like Rose disliked dogs, and who could blame her knowing the history. In the past, they had her running for her life. Rose had once been chased and attacked by a huge dog, that resembled a bear. Thank God, the owners came out to rescue her, after her uncontrollable screaming could be heard from even beyond the grave. So there`s no way Rose was going to allow such a thing to recur again, having the day that she`s had. Shouting her sister's name again,, she was suddenly filled with so much melancholy, flowing through her veins it was overwhelming to bear.

The tears came rolling down her face like a fountain, it was seemingly impossible to console her. Rose shouted Maria`s name again and again. "Maria, Maria, Maria," her cries becoming more and more desperate. Maria came running through the door, with the most astonished look on her face. As she got closer to Rose, her sister could see how devasted she was. "What`s wrong? Did someone die"? She kept asking question after question, before even receiving the first answer. She held Rose's hand and took her into the house, hoping that she would get some answers soon. "So what's wrong" she asked again.

"Hum! Rose responded, "Oh, how I wish that I were dead," she kept repeating to herself. They walked towards a double bedroom, that had two single beds inside. There was an old woman wearing a floral dress sitting up, sipping on a teacup which she held with one hand. The bed was shoved closely to a wall, as if to prevent her from falling through the cracks. She was trying to get out of bed, but Rose could see that she was struggling. Maria, stopped to assist the woman who appeared to be grateful, as if saying thanks wasn't enough. By this time Rose had refrained from crying, but her eyes were still puffy.

"Are you alright dear," the old woman asked, smiling kindly. "I`ll be OK" Rose answered vaguely. The woman then looked at her and said, "don't worry, things will get better," as she sat sipping her tea and chatting to Maria about how she was going to the chicken coop that day.

Maria introduced the old woman as Granny, but her real name was Miss Edith. She was tall, slender and her complexion was like caramel. She was looking cross but had a warm attitude about her. Surprisingly, she was quite friendly, and her voice was as strong as wailing elephant, but was as harmless as a lamb.

Maria had two sons; the oldest one, Kevin, from a previous relationship, wasn't living with her at the time. He was living with Rose`s dad and mother in the country since he was, a baby and was like a little brother to them. His great love for food was fascinating. Rose remembers one time when Kevin was about eight years old, and he and his cousin Kelly, who was also being brought up by Rose's parent, were misbehaving and so their grandmother, decided to teach them a lesson. It was around dinner time that Miss Jane went for the belt and started hitting Kevin. He just kept on eating, bawling with the food still in his mouth. Kelly was different; she wasn't going to eat while getting hit by a belt. She tossed the food upon for the floor and ran to hide.

Maria's youngest son, Peter, who was then about three years old, was sound asleep when Rose arrived, but not long after he was awakened. He looked nothing like Kevin, which wasn't surprising considering that they had different dads, but nevertheless he was sweet; could tell he was a lovely boy. He had the complexion of his granny. By this time Rose was feeling hungry and exhausted from her long journey. Her sister had a small grocery shop in their yard, more like a supermarket in the community. Dinner wasn't ready yet ,so Rose brought a bun and a slice of cheese from the shop to catch up her stomach. She ate it down quickly and drink a bottle of water, it felt like she hadn't eaten for days.

After Rose finish eating her snacks, she went around the back of the yard where Maria was sitting down under the shade of a big mango tree. It had large branches, that were hanging down to the ground, the mangoes dangling, as if it were a Christmas tree, decorated with beautiful lights, except, of course, they were delicious mangoes waiting to be eaten. Under the tree was a wooden bench, that had the capacity for two to three people to sit on. They sat together, under the mango tree. Rose stared into space as if she were reliving the event that had brought her here all over again. Eventually she broke her silence, revealing, to her sister what had transpired, leading up to the what had happened that morning, leaving her no choice but to run away, from their parents 'home. Maria borrowed a friend's phone, so she could call their parents to inform them that Rose was safe and was staying at her house for the time being. It was almost dinner time. Rose's sister got up from the bench and went into the kitchen. She started to prepare the ingredients for dinner.

"Is there anything I could do?" Rose asked her,. "No, it's OK. You`ve had a long day". "But you can stay here with me if you like," and she gestured towards a small chair in the corner of the kitchen, so

Rose pulled it close and sat down. A few moment later Rose, got up and went outside the kitchen into the yard. She wanted to look at the surrounding area, after so many years of not being there.

Rose noticed an old man she hadn't met before approaching her from the back room of the house. He was tall and carried a wooden stick with him, as if it was his chaperone. It was obvious his health was failing slowly, but that did not stop him from being mobile. He seemed a little frail but strong enough to get about on his own. He focused his attention on Rose.

"Hello young miss," how are you doing." Rose was surprised as she didn't know someone else was living in the house. "Oh, sorry, "she hesitated. "I`m Maria's sister, Rose. Nice to meet you," she saw the resemblance; knew straight away he was related to Ricky. "Everyone calls me Grandfather", otherwise known as Albert, he said walking closer towards Rose. He kept looking at her as if his sight was impaired even though, he was wearing glasses. She smiled at him as he continued to speak. He showed such gracefulness, you could almost see into this soul. He spoke of the fruit trees, like he wished he was one of them himself. She just stood there allowing him, to enjoy the company of his new acquaintance. After a while he walked away slowly, as if he had forgotten something. " Yeah! I`ll see you later, young miss."" OK grandfather I'll look forward to it," Rose said.

Sharlene who hadn't been home when Rose arrived came back from school later that evening, . She was Maria's stepdaughter; Ricky had two children from previous relationships, but his son only came on occasional visits. The dogs were wagging their tails on her arrival, jumping around her with excitement. She treated the dogs well, always making sure that they were fed, and so did the others. Rose could see why the family loved Sharlene,; she had a graceful presence about her, polite and confident. Rose had met her some time ago, but she spent a lot of time at her mother's back then. As she walked toward the veranda Rose, smiled at her.

"Hello," she greeted Rose with a surprised look on her face. "How are you?" Rose asked her."

Give me a few seconds, yeah?" she said over her shoulder as she went looking for Maria in the kitchen, to say good evening. The kitchen was built on the house, so it was hard finding anyone. Her voice could be heard throughout the house. "Evening granny" she continued. Rose was intrigue with her mannerism. Sharlene appear energetic, like she`d never had a dull day, and it was refreshing to have her around. Her appearance was rather petite. She then went and changed from her school uniform into her regular clothes. By now it was dinner time, Maria called Sharlene and Rose to the kitchen to assist her, by taking the plates of food into the house. Grandfather came out from his bedroom when Sharlene shouted his name to come to the dinner table, although occasionally he would eat in his room. Granny came to the table. she, too, had a walking stick, she seemed to be taller than Rose had at first imagined, and she stares at her, impressed. Everyone was there including Ricky, chatting, and eating. Rose realised that they all, had strong personalities and maybe clashed sometimes. How interesting! She sighed as she listened to them sharing their difference of opinions. Ricky, Rose believed had the strongest character of them all. "I can see where Sharlene inherits her genes from," Rose nodded, staring at them.

Everything was as expected, and they got on well, considering their personalities. Depending on the topics they were discussing, their hopes and ambitions came out. Ricky had a brother, Rodney, who lived in a small cottage in the yard, and who was quite the odd one, scary most of the times. Rose didn't know him even though they resided in the same yard, as he mostly kept to himself. It was evident they didn't share the same father because granddad wasn't his father. Rodney had one son, Tony, who had suffered mentally, and he was just there like a lost sheep with no one to find him. In those days people's ignorance towards mental health was crippling, on top of their superstitious behaviour. Tony`s dad, Rodney, was no different from the strangers they walked amongst, and was probably the meanest towards him. Rose regarded his present, but at first was intimidated by his appearance. eventually she realised that he just wanted to survive like everyone else did. Sometimes for days, he would disappear, they had often anticipated his death, but he had always returned, rising like a phoenix from the ashes. Maria offered him food whenever she could, and he was grateful but his favourite meal was, bizarrely, half a loaf of bread and some sugar. "Miss Rose," he shouted, "Can I beg you for a little sugar, please," but before she could reply he was standing in front of her with his metal container. Days became weeks, weeks became months, and finally the day came when Maria planned a trip to go visit their parents. Rose's mood changed immediately, the fear of seeing her father again almost crippling her.

The thought of seeing her dad was over exhausting, and she hoped that he would be sober. If he was intoxicated she wouldn't be responsible for what might happen. If in another life, she told herself, gazing into the distant skies. Rose was hoping for a miracle of some type, that would mean they couldn't go. She hoped, maybe the van would develop a technical fault and couldn't be driven. "Maria I don't think I want to come with you guys tomorrow", she said, looking serious.

"Why," her sister asked.

"Are you really asking me that," questioned Rose, feeling frustrated at Maria.

It's been ages since you left. He should be happy to see you"

"Oh God! That man will never let go; he`s like a baby elephant – badly behaved and never forgets," Rose replied as she walked off."

Her sister went after her. "Honestly, Rose, I didn't mean to freak you out. I know what you've being through. Watching you suffer in silence. That dark mark on your thigh, I notice that, too," Maria cried. Oh thanks! I wasn't sure you cared that much, Rose mumbled under her breath. At times Rose, felt alone because no one talked about the stuff that had happened in the past; everything, seemed to be shoved aside, leaving her to sort her feelings out on her own. It was the longest night Rose had ever experienced; she was unable to sleep, tossing and turning, as if someone had place her in a barrel and rolled her down a hill.

The day for the visit finally arrived. Ricky, used his company van, to make the journey which a triumphant one. It was Sunday morning, and so the traffic was minimal,; smooth sailing all the way. They had an early breakfast, showered and got dressed, and all too soon they were ready. It was a pleasant journey, filled with laughter and excitement for some; but for Rose, it was sheer torture, full of fear of unknown. When they got to the house Rose was the last one to exit the van. Everyone was at home when they arrived; her dad was assisting the animals to drink water from a white bucket. Rose pretended not to see him, considering he was focusing on the job in hand, so she quickly slipped into the house. she was excited to see her younger siblings, just as they were at seeing her; they shouted her name in excitement. Rose hugged her mom.

"You're looking well dear, her mother said with a smile of relief on her face.

"Really good to see you, too, mama. How are you doing?

I'm doing OK she replied. Rose went outside to be with her siblings, who were waiting anxiously to hear what had happened to her the day she left. She explained as much as she could, under the circumstances. Her dad did not speak to her throughout the entire visit. Rose didn't seem to care; her only concern was that he wasn't hammered. She was alright, and so she made sure to stay out of his way until it was time to leave. It was now getting dark and time to go Ricky said, so everyone said their goodbyes. Rose was deeply sad and was quiet for most of the journey home. All that she could think about was her mom and siblings; leaving them behind was hard for her. 'God, please watch over my mother and sisters, for me and keep them safe' she prayed, being filled with dismay at what they still might be suffering at the hands of that man. Rose was angry at her mother for a while because she had never defended her, didn't even try. She often wondered why was she so weak, but one doesn't know what goes on in peoples' minds. Suddenly Rose realised that maybe she couldn't; she had always seemed frightened of him. It took her sometime to figure out what made sense to her, so that she could move on with her life. Rose's mother got her full share of turmoil, and that, too, was another factor in finding forgiveness for her.

After a few days Ricky, came home from work informing Rose that he had got her a job. It was with his brother's wife in Kingston.

Rose would often help Maria in her grocery shop and she was surprisingly good at it. She was living in Maria's home, eating and drinking with no money to pay her way so this was her contribution towards the household expenses. But Maria couldn't afford to Rose a wage, and since she was living there, she needed a job to buy her necessities. Evidently, getting paid employment was the only solution. Rose was feeling positive about it. They talked about it on several occasion, but now the reality of Kingston had arrived. Eventually the day came and Rose was feeling very nervous. Ricky assured her it wasn't that dreadful in Kingston; he knew because he had driven there nearly every day for many years. Rose rolled her eyes, but he didn't notice; the stories she had heard that were told about Kingston by many people she knew were sometimes jaw dropping.

"Are you sure it's going to be alright," Rose questioned him. Ricky appeared puzzled, but then he started laughing, and said "You`ll be alright, Besides you`ll be coming home after work every day". The journey was a long one, and Rose had mixed reactions knowing how she tended to overthink everything. When they got there it was early. Ricky had to go to his own job. He quickly introduced her to them and then he was gone. Ms Peg was Ricky`s sister-in-law, Buggy`s wife, and the owner of the restaurant. She explained to Rose about the daily routines and what her role would be working at the restaurant. She also introduced Rose to some of the employees who worked for her. The day went well for Rose, especially meeting Pauline, Ms Peg daughter. They were the same in age, making it easier for Rose to relate to her, and besides, Pauline seemed friendly enough.

CHAPTER 5
THE UNKNOWN CITY

After Rose started working at the restaurant, she occasionally had to continue with her journey on her own, by catching the bus to her workplace when Ricky was unable to drop her off. Sometimes she would be late for work, due to the morning rush. Ms Peg, wasn't happy about Rose coming in late but would not say anything. Her facial expression would speak volumes, as if to say, 'Why are you late again?' She was short, a little stocky, had sleepy eyes and seemed tired all the time, and often muttered under her breath. Rose hated it when she did that. Anyway, she thought the poor woman was over-exhausted from all the years of working hard. No wonder she behaved so on edge all the time. Ricky's brother had a strange nickname, Buggy. Everyone called him that but Rose thought it was a safe bet that wasn't his real name, even though he acted as if that was the name given him by his mom. He was tall and slim, of caramel complexion, and he swore a lot, quite loudly. He never knew what time of day it was, from being intoxicated with alcohol, so different to his brother, Ricky. He had a motor bike; he would ride it even when he was drunk, weaving from side to side like a cyclist riding on a rainy day. God only knew how he survived that long; he probably thought he was superhuman. The funny thing was that he would often pick fights with people he was familiar with. Rose never saw that one coming; the epitome of her dad, a reminder of what she had left behind. She never expected that it would resurface so soon. How contrary!

Ms Peg was always appeared to be agitated and uneasy; whenever Buggy was wasted he became unpredictable. She was no match for him; he could be intimidating, making you wish that you were invisible. All her secrets would now be heard, anything that she told him in confidence about any of her staff; All the things she didn't have the nerve to say to them to their faces, would come tumbling out. That was always so embarrassing for Ms Peg. Rose always tried to be close enough so that she could see her reaction. He would be shouting loudly; his natural voice tone was of a high pitch so that came easy to him; he didn't have to try very hard. Everyone heard him. "You don't have the balls to be upfront to anyone; you are such a hypocrite. All you do is moan about your staff", then the fireworks would begin. Some of the things he would say would be shocking. Ms Peg, would just keep silent; not a word would she utter in her own defence. After a while Ricky, was not driving so much to work; he was working less days so they decided that it would be better if Rose stayed in Kingston. That meant living with the people that she worked for. This was going to be challenging after knowing so much about Ms Peg, and Buggy.

Well, finally the day came when Rose, went to live in Kingston. She was scared to leave Maria`s home even though they had their ups and downs, but it was nothing comparing to what was going to happen next. It took her a while to get used to living with Ms Peg and her family, but what choice did she have? She could go back to live in the country with her dad, or live with people who were almost strangers to her. Oh well how hard could it be? Pauline welcomed Rose with open arms and so did the rest of the family. They were already familiar with each other, so Rose knew something of what to expect. Pauline and Rose were about the same age and it made a world of difference having her there.

They both had children from previous relationships: Buggy, had about six children with another woman and Ms Peg had two children from a previous relationship, too. What was remarkably shocking was that Ms Peg, had five children with Buggy who were the same age as his other children from his previous relationship. Rose couldn't wrap her head around that; it meant he must have been living a double life. Rose was used to a different sort of life; despite their shortcomings her own mom and dad's eight children were all from their relationship together., But as strange as it was, she didn't want to be judgemental. Later Rose learnt that the siblings from both sides were rivals in one way or the other, and that Buggy's other children resented Ms Peg, deeply, or at least most of them did. They all had their own problems and dramas that never seemed to end; every day there was something new. Rose often thought that life couldn't have been any crueller, and wondered why God had forsaken her; why could this not be a normal family? But then again, maybe normal would be very boring.

Pauline she was quiet and kept to herself but not in a bad way. She had a chocolate complexion and was of medium build. You could tell that she looked after her hair and she was quite pleasant and somewhat friendly in her own way. Rose discovered they had a lot in common, and over time they became close friends; they shared the same room but slept in different beds. They started to confide in each other and that was the first time Rose started to feel that she belonged. Pauline was kind, but she could be a little lazy where work was concerned. She didn't have a specific job or profession, but would occasionally assist in the restaurant if she desired to do so. Pauline appeared to get on with everyone that worked in her mother's restaurant. They all liked her, and it helped that she was the boss's daughter, but Rose saw much more than that in her. Pauline was an honest person and genuinely looked out for Rose like a sister would and so Rose returned the same value towards her. Apart from Ms Peg being responsible for Pauline, she also had close family members who were living in USA at the time. They would support her with money and clothing. Rose was never jealous of her but would sometimes wish there were someone else apart from herself, assisting her now and then. That would be nice.

They had two other children living at the house: Ms Peg's grandchildren, Suzan and Malley. Sometimes they would be with Ms Peg and sometimes they stayed at their mom's house; Rose didn't understand much about the arrangement. Their dad, Ms Peg`s son was living in the USA the time.

The restaurant that Ms Peg owned also had some small houses at the back of it and these were occupied by people who worked for her in the restaurant. Rose, herself, was living in their family home, shared by Pauline, Buggy, Ms Peg and her two grandchildren. After all Ricky and Buggy were brothers, and that was the right thing for them to do. It was odd for her, living with strangers. She had to adapt and get on with it. Living with, and working for someone can be hard work; you are treated differently, even if they are being genuine that is just how it works. At some point, you realise that you are not free, only in your mind, so you often remind yourself of the whole purpose of why you are there. There were five people working in the restaurant excluding Rose, and at one time she was the only female working there for a while. Rose felt so alone and lost. This is not my world. I do not belong here. So many doubts going through her mind; even in her sleep she heard herself thinking. Each day came with something new; for Rose, she would frequently think about her own family that she had left behind, especially her siblings, who she missed veery much.

They had a close bond with each other, especially her younger siblings and it was difficult being so far away from them. This wasn't what she had dreamt of, after leaving school, working in a place, so far away from home. Kingston wouldn't have been her initial choice. Rose had always been passionate about writing, it was her escape into a different dimension, a world where she felt safe and at peace. A place that no one could invade or touch, it was her haven. She wrote songs, poems, and sometimes even short stories, and reminiscing, she had to hold back the tears. Oh, how I miss those days: writing my songs and singing them in church with my siblings, and at harvests time. Her youngest sister, Jenna, who would have been about eight at this time, was so brave that she could have stood before a million people without fear She was the cutest little person you could ever see, and looking back, those days seemed blissful and bright. Now what she was feeling was darkness, loneliness and an emptiness that did not seem to go away. Rose believed in her dreams and hoped that one day she would be a great writer or singer, and would be the savour for her siblings. Eventually she started settling in her new home and that took a long while, but it was enough to start with.

Rose, routine had added responsibilities that were placed upon her, but she was not ready for this, it was way too early. This wasn't fair. Why did she have to face all this extra pressure; waking up every morning as early as the sun would rise in the sky, but Rose had no choice in the matter. Where they were living was even scary to walk during the daytime, not to mention at night. A prayer was your only option, if you did not know how, or your overactive mind would surely drive you insane. For a country girl like Rose who had not been permitted to even go to the neighbour's house, this was too much to handle. Hearing the stories about Kingston, everyone was terrified during those days; no one would dare travelled to such a place unless they had no choice. The stories were even worse than it really was; Rose convinced herself of that reality to save herself. For those that were living in Kingston already knew of its danger and probably accepted that way of life. Either that or they were they pretending to be brave.

Some mornings were nerve-racking, given that it was still dark and no sunshine to guide her path, all she had were electrical post lights in the distance. Ms Peg had a son who slept on the floor in the restaurant, even though she gave him a room in the property, and he was always awake to open the doors of the restaurant so that they could enter. He was creepy, often making Rose uncomfortable. She had to keep a straight face whenever he was around; smiling wouldn't be a natural thing to do as he would take it as an invitation to be acting inappropriately. Rose didn't trust him, and surely avoided him in every way she could. She later learnt that he too was afraid of the area. Whatever it was that he was terrified of, that was his reason for hiding in the restaurant. 'Thank god I'm not the only one who is scared of this sinister danger surrounding the area,' Rose thought to herself. At one time she might have been scared of ghosts in the dark, but here it was not visitors from the spirit world that made her afraid. Now the wheels had turned, and even in daylight she was terrified of what men might be capable of doing.

The road that led to their house, was a dirt lane filled with bushes and trees on one side of the pathway, and a massive high wall on the opposite side. From the steepness of the wall Rose guessed that it must be hiding some sort of restricted security building. Beyond the wall was a boat factory that was used for building fishing boats – 'Well that is something you don't see every day, Rose thought. When Rose first came here this scenery was all new to Rose; where she came from you would not see things like that so commonly. Leaving the community and travelling to town, the views were different. She worked long hours at the restaurant, from seven in the morning until five in the evening. That meant most of the other workers would be going home to their families, but not Rose. At five o'clock she would be going home to have a shower, change and returned for the night shift.

The night shift would begin at six and finished at eleven o'clock, or sometimes later. For Rose it felt she like was living in a bubble, going round and round in a never-ending nightmare. She would often prepare fried chicken, and cook rice and peas, then assist with serving it to the customers. She was always exhausted, but never complained. In her mind she knew it wasn't right but who was she going to tell. Pauline would sometimes help in the restaurant by serving the customers or working at the till, so Rose could take a break. Rose was grateful to be earning her own money it gave her independence, but she knew that she deserved better. She told herself one day she would be somebody, and that all these things were only temporary. Rose did what she had to, surviving and promising herself not to be entrapped in that world.

It's better than nothing, Lord, and I'm not been ungrateful, but I believe that better days are ahead. If this makes me a bad person, then my faith is sealed into your hands," she prayed as she looked to the skies.

Normally some of the guys who worked for Ms Peg, would return during the night to accompany them home. Rose found solace and comfort, knowing that it would be safer than walking down the dirt road on her own in the middle of the night. Then one night there were no bodyguards (that was what Rose thought of them as). They weren't around that night. It was about twelve o'clock, everything seemed bright, as Rose and the other three people walked home.. Ms Peg was the leader, as usual taking charge of the front-line. Rose would normally be walking in the middle or at the back, as she felt safer there. The moon was beaming down brightly, it was crystal clear she kept watching her shadow as they maintained their pace down the pathway. The eeriness felt like the ghost on Christmas eve. Rose was tired; all she could think of was getting home and going to bed. Suddenly Ms Peg stopped in the pathway. She was saying something but Rose was unable to hear her, probably because she was too far behind. It was like driving a car in traffic, and suddenly someone stops in front of you without signalling. The impact felt strange, confusing thoughts going through her mind – that's how Rose felt. They were hiding behind the trees; three masked bandits came out from amongst the bushes with weapon of mass destruction ready to take what wasn't theirs. They forced Ms Peg's face towards the massive wall, and ordered everyone else to do the same. The leader then proceeded to demand Ms Peg's money. At the bottom of the wall sharp thorns were growing on the ground, and everyone was been pricked and scratched on their bodies. It was a night of doom: no one knew what their fate was going to be, Rose felt paralysed. She managed to pray a little prayer to come out alive and that no one would be hurt, or worse.

Rose was frantic, she thought that her whole world was coming to an end, even the smell from the dirt track was getting stronger, than it usually was, the air, too, had a different odour; she thought it was the smell of death. It was the first time in a long while that she wished that she was home with her own family; she would prefer being beaten by her dad than this. As she turned her head around to look at one of the masked men, one of them was standing closer than she thought. He held a gun to her face and said in a deep harsh voice, "harlot, turn your face to the wall and stop looking at me or I'll give you something to really look at". Rose nervously turned her head away quickly in despair, facing the wall. Nothing could prepare Rose, for what was about to unfold in the next few minutes of that night. During the commotion Bugg, was riding his motor bike, on his way home, and was just riding down through that dusty, old, dirt lane. He was totally unaware that his family were being robbed at that moment of time. There was not a streetlight in sight, because it was not a regular street and only the light of the moon beamed through the darkness of the night, casting a dim light. From where he was on his motor bike, Buggy, was too far away to see what was happening to his family, further up the lane.

When the men heard the approach of the unsuspecting Buggy one of the gang fired two shots in the direction of the oncoming motorbike. They heard the roar of the engine that had been echoing in the distance suddenly stop no sound of its roaring engine, no light in sight, nothing. Everything seemed to be frozen in time, and everyone was as silent as if they had been walking through a graveyard. Reality was slipping away, and insanity was now taking over their minds, including Roses, as she was going through her first encounter with robbers. Suddenly, Pauline screamed out her father's name with ever fibre she had left in her body. They waited and waited but no answer came back through the stillness of the dark. All this time the thieves had continued to find the hidden money on Ms Peg, although she had already told them that there was none. The presumptuous thieves, continued by frisking everyone in the hope of finding the money, but their luck was out. Eventually they ran off towards the trees and bushes, disappearing into the tranquillity of the night. Rose had no thought of reality; her mind went blank. It felt like a maze, but she couldn't find her way out, instead she just stood there like a zombie.

Eventually everyone seemed to gather themselves together with the glimmer of hope that Buggy might be still alive. All feet thundering down the path towards the direction of the once oncoming motorbike. they got to the top of the dirt road Buggy, was nowhere in sight, he was gone. They all wondered, and in the worse possible way, about what could have happened to him, and why he was he not there. They looked closely all around on where his motorbike was laying on the ground to see if there were any blood stain, but nothing was there either. As they continue with their quest in search of the missing body or person, they were walking toward the high road. He saw them coming and came out of his hiding place, trembling like a leaf on a branch on a windy day; he had a blank stare in his eyes as if he were in a different time. Ms Peg and the others were ecstatic to have found him and were more overjoyed that he wasn't hurt, but only frightened and shaken. Rose has never seen him lost for words before but on that night, he was. They walked back home together, Buggy picked up his bike, mounted it and rode home without the echo of its mighty roar. The others all walked home that night in total silence; no one said a word. Rose wondered if the masked men were still lurking in the dark, and she felt the thrill of horror ran down the back of her spine.

It was late when they got home, Rose was still overwhelmed with fear from the terrible ordeal, she wondered what everyone else was thinking, even though she already knew the answer. She didn't see the need to say anything about what happened, and so she went to bed. Throughout the night, Rose was unable to close her eyes, all that she could see when she closed her eyes was the attack occurring all over again. The morning came faster than ever, everything seemed and felt different. Ms Peg's eyes were puffy and red, due to lack of sleep they could tell she was still in shock. She got up earlier than usual the following morning which proved the poor woman hadn't slept. Her movements were slightly off, but she was able to get ready for work, business as usual. Pauline was up, to, She was always a late sleeper, but this time she, too was out of bed. Boggy, was sitting on the sofa in their living room, reading some old newspaper. Rose, stared at him and thought to herself, this must be a distraction for this old catfish, he wasn't reading anything just gazing on the pages, as if he were reading the headline of the attack in the papers. As for Rose, whatever, she felt at the time couldn't be explained, was a mixture of confusion and illusion. She told herself that probably, it was a horrible nightmare, and so she tried her best to remain calm, something she knew very well how to do. Rose created a tiny world in her mind, one that no one could enter unless they were invited. However only a handful of select people were given that chance to enter; those were her chosen.

Ms Peg told everyone that the thieves did not get the money that they were searching so desperately for, as she had hidden it on her body. It was unbelievable how she did it; when she explained in detail to Rose, who, she thought to herself, must have had years of experiences to disguise something like that. Ms Peg was a veteran in the business, a living, breathing icon. You must learn survival skills, or you would get lost in the battle, or be swallowed up like shark a, swallowing tiny fishes in the deep. By then everyone was at work, and the incident that transpired on that dreadful nigh, was the topic for the day. Everyone was playing detective but had no clue as to what happened because they were not there. Rose did not say much but she listened intently to everyone's opinions and theories. Some thought it was a setup from perhaps one of the workers, while others believed differently.

The robbery wasn't reported to the police. Rose was astonished and thought how strange that was, but maybe that was their way of doing things, and besides, no one was killed, and Ms Peg still had most of her money. The memory left Rose paralyzed in her mind and thought nothing would ever be the same again. There and then Rose knew that wasn't the life she wanted for herself. For a couple of weeks it was all they talked about, until finally there was nothing more to say about it, like an old forgotten tale. The idea of being so vulnerable was not resting well with Rose; she was terrified of being caught up the fireworks again. She was worried they`d come back again and hurt someone badly nor even me, maybe her and how would her family bear such dreadful news. Although Pauline and Ms Peg tried to reassure her that she would be OK, Rose wasn't able to find comfort in their words. It became obvious to Rose that this was not the first time such a thing had occurred, and that thought was devastating. She guessed they might get their full share of thieves; she did understand that it couldn't be easy for any of them, that this did not come with a manual book.

"Where I`m from, people can sleep with their doors open, and our neighbours would close it for you, if that was ever the case, but here in Kingston, Pauline, it's horrendous," Rose told her friend. Rose felt like she was caught up in a world of violence, with cold blooded murderers who wouldn't think twice if you stood in their way. 'What would my life be, if I had stayed in the country with my parents, Rose thought as she watched a flock of birds flying overhead, looking so free. Her pain was a constant reminder, of her past as she felt nothing but loneliness,; she felt like it was always some dilemma waiting to occur. She'd never seen a weapon in her life before, and now everywhere she looked she saw men walking around armed day and night, like they were living in the Wild West. Some were educated apparently, high school A Star student. What happened to make them like this, only God knows, their fall has no boundary. Thieves, pick pockets, grabbing handbags you name it, they did it; they were callous, and cold-hearted, Rose thought. They saw their actions as doing what was necessary to survive;, Rose saw them as extortionist, robbing from poor people they didn't care about; surely not Robin Hood.

The weeks had become months now and Rose decided that she would go and visit her sister, Maria, every other weekend. She needed that escape because she sometimes felt like a prisoner, trapped and worried most of the time. The weekends would often seem too brief. Rose would come up with excuses to stay a few days longer at her sister's house. At this point she didn't care much about what Ms Peg thought of the situation anymore. At that time a few of the workers left the job at the restaurant, so Ms Peg had to hire a few new members of staff. Some of them were locals and they all seemed to know their way around the area. Eventually the robbery became a thing of the past, very few words were spoken about it, it was gone in the wind.

They say lightning doesn't strike twice in the same place, and surely that's a myth; one that keeps you in balance so you won't go crazy. It was Wednesday night about 9pm, and was just getting dark; nothing out of the ordinary, the same routine as usual. The thing with evil is that it occurs when you`re most vulnerable, when you are caught up in the moment, and you least expect it. Little did Rose know that danger was lurking in the darkness. Pauline was sitting on the back porch of the restaurant with her nephew and niece, and Rose was sitting at the customer counter looking at the passers-by. Ms Peg was in her tiny office, with the door half open., In the meantime Buggy was being his usual charming self, hammered as hell. Unexpectedly Pauline, ran past pulling her nephew like a rag doll, everything was happening so fast Rose was mesmerised. She moved swiftly towards the door, to find some logical explanation for her strange behaviour, but poor Rose wasn't fast enough. Someone grabbed her by the back of her shirt neck, and pushed something hard into her side, pulling her backwards. She then realised what was happening. They were standing in Ms Peg office, and that`s when Rose realised that it was a firearm that she could feel.

Rose was livid, with a mixture of fear and confusion, how could this be possible she thought as she observed what was happening. This time there were two of them, masked gunmen, one of them holding a gun at Ms Peg head. Buggy was swearing at them none stop but to no avail. Rose looked around the old grey room that only had death written on the walls, 'I must be hallucinating' Rose sighed to herself, watching Ms Peg, as she held her head down without a word in her defence. The night went by slowly, giving the thieves ample time to carry out their plot, and this time they weren't leaving without the money. Ms Peg had now become a target, Rose for the second time in a year. Rose believed that was no coincidence; it was a highly planned operation carried out by people who never worked a day in their lives. Staring death in the face, she felt nothing, all her senses vanishing gradually.

"I guess this is what dying feels like," she kept saying over and over in her mind. The robber's odour was unpleasant, like they`d been hiding out in the green bushes. A couple of weeks before, a nearby grocery shop had been robbed, and the owner killed. Ms Peg was shaking, petrified; the look on her face was like she was having a breakdown. They took the money from Ms Peg, walking away without a care in the world, vanishing the way they came. About half an hour after the robbers had left , a few of the guys that worked at the restaurant came by, but there was nothing they could do; the damage was already done. At first, she couldn't comprehend what had happened. She felt like her soul had left her body, and as she stood staring into oblivion. watching her soul float around, she thought to herself ,'well I`m officially dead!', Then Pauline came back, too, and she rested her hand around Rose's shoulder, gesturing for her to sit down, giving her a cup of water to drink. Rose slowly sipped it without even knowing what she was doing. It finally dawned on her that she was in shock, a rebirth with much perception. Buggy was now stone-cold sober; it was unbelievable how quickly he recovered from his drunken condition. Ms Peg asked the guys to help her close the restaurant. She was still shaking like a leaf on a windy day. It didn't take long; they closed up, and then everyone went home.

It was the same as before – the police weren't informed about the incident. It was difficult for Rose to understand at first: it made no sense to her whatsoever. She was afraid it was too complicated to handle. Ms Peg, had no names, no faces, but strongly everyone has the same unwavering belief. For days Ms Peg appeared unwell. Some mornings she was unable to get out of bed, and Pauline and Rose had to cover for her. As much as Rose believed Ms Peg was been victimized, and thought she was handling it well, she could see the effect was extremely trying for her. Rose was still processing the 'what ifs' in her mind; but despite everything, at least everyone was still alive, and still had a chance to start again.

" Pauline, I`m taking some time off," Rose said, pausing between words she smiled tensely, holding back her tears. ran

"Sorry I didn't warn you, they were coming, Rose," Pauline said. "I just panicked and ran."

"It`s no one's fault, especially not yours" Rose replied, tapping her shoulders, ensuring her clarity.

Both talked for a while about what happened. Pauline was the only one who knew how Rose felt, "When are you leaving?" she asked softly.

"I`ll go later in the evening. It`s just for a week though," she gasped!

"It's going to be alright, Rose. It took me a long time too to overcome my fear, too. After a while you start feeling paralysed, frightened of everything that moves. By adapting to the fact you're still alive, it gives you hope that one day things will change, so I know".

Rose was lost for words, all along she assumed it, but now it was real sigh!

"I`m so sorry Pauline, I feel so selfish, Oh how awful of me!"

Rose recognised that they were victims, trying to survive, hoping for change. The weekend came and Rose went away to visit her family. She carried on as best as she knew how. Feeling sorry for herself wouldn't be the right thing for her mental state.

A few years had passed and Rose started to feel stagnant like a river that had no flow, nowhere to go. Even though she was happy with herself and had few good people in her corner, there was always a void that couldn't be filled. Having those feelings was like constantly fighting a demon, but a good one that constantly reminded her of her purpose. It kept telling her that she needed to fight, to do better and achieve what she was placed on this earth for. Rose had ambition and drive; deep down she wanted to make her family proud and to show them that she could be someone, even though they were not there for her. She always dreamt of being a nurse day one, caring for people was a natural essence about her. Rose believed that no matter where you are from or whoever you are, that should not limit a one's ability to excel and be the best version of oneself you can be. If life throws you a brick do not stay knock down by it, pick yourself up and start again – that was the motto for her survival. She also knew that times were hard for a lot of people, and not everyone was able to save; not even a penny; some people could hardly survive, and the little they had was given to support their family.

Over time Rose, saved a few thousand dollars from her earnings; she hid it in the corner of her raggedy old suitcase that she kept under the bed. She had slept on it for years; not even the ants would find it. The day finally came when Rose decided to use her rainy-day cash. It took her a while to decide. Knowing that it was all the savings she had in the world, but still she knew it was the right thing to do. She prayed about it for several days; she was always a great believer in God, knowing that he would show her the right path. Eventually she applied to a nursing school in Kingston; something that she wanted to do for years. She was excited and believed that her dream was finally coming through; no matter what happen from then on it would be worth it. Rose worked during the day and attended classes in the evening. It was hard, but she was determined to make a change in her life, to be somebody. She felt important; her colleagues at work supported and respected her, especially so, her friend Pauline. She was doing great and was enjoying her new beginning, being taught things that she had only dreamt of, was now becoming a reality; that empty void was starting to be filled.

The thought of being someone who people respected and looked up to gave Rose a greater purpose and desire to want it even more. The course was for a year, and Rose was now six-months into her studies, exploring and enjoying it as best as she could. At times she was tired from the long days of working in the restaurant but that could not stop her. A few months later, an incident occurred between Ricky and Buggy; family matters they said it was, but for some reason they could not reach an understanding. As far as Rose was concerned it was their problem; after all they were brothers. At one time when they were arguing, it was like having two male lions roaring for power and neither was backing down. Ricky was a decent person, never really swore or used indecent language, while on the other hand Buggy was doing it for both of them. It did not become physical between them, so there was still hope that whenever they decided to make amends hopefully the doors would be open. Rose was lost in thoughts over the next few days; she felt uneasy about the brotherly division. 'What will the outcome be for me, she thought, 'even worse to be still living with them, especially that discontented old owl.

She related her concerns to Pauline, who was looking more confused than ever. Rose burst out laughing,

"Sorry. This is a serious matter but the look on your face, I had to laugh, otherwise I would not know where to begin. Listen, this is not your fault so stop looking so deflated. No matter what happens, we will remain friends forever, OK", she said. She continued with her jokes, "girl the way your big eyes are popping, it reminded me of when a deer gets caught in the headlights" They both burst out laughing.

"You are funny," Pauline said to Rose. She continued,, "let's go sit down on the veranda. Its lovely out there", and so they did. As they sat together Rose, started to talk she laid everything out, nothing was left unsaid. She spoke with such a calmness in her voice, she didn't want Pauline to believe that she was upset with her when in fact she wasn't. Pauline listened attentively without saying much. She was incredibly supportive towards Rose, and she tried to reassure her that the issue between her dad and Ricky would not affect her working or living with them, but Rose was not so sure, even though she accepted Pauline's words. Whenever Buggy was intoxicated he would argue about Ricky, saying things that were mean and untrue. Life is so unfair when someone isn't around to defend their honour. Rose would shake her head with disbelieve. She felt so clumsy whenever he was around; her energy felt so forced and strained. 'Really, how dare you! Trying to ruin my dream that I've worked so hard for.' she thought to herself, 'when I got nothing to do with your sibling affair'. His constant rumbling and bickering was starting to affect Rose. The psychological, pressure was intensifying, making it difficult for her to even study. At times, his outburst would sound like a personal attack on her.

Rose's studies were being threatened. It was becoming a habit for him, to be intoxicated almost every day. Ms Peg would just sit in her tiny office looking lost, as if she had been traveling into another dimension. Her money drawer would be half open, and she would be sleeping; she always seemed so tired just watching her nodding would break your heart, to even just look at her. Considering that Ms Peg has being exposed and embarrassed so often by her drunken husband's behaviour; it was evident that she did not want to be involved in his little charade. One could not blame her for trying in her endeavour to avoid him in every way she could. Moreover it never did end very well for her.

As luck would have it, Rose met this woman at the restaurant. She could tell that she was in her late twenties, she had a caramel complexion, was short, but what struck Rose most was her resemblance to one of Rose`s dad's far cousins. It was remarkable. . Rose and her would exchange a brief 'hello' at first, but eventually they got the know each other. Her name was Charmaine; she was pleasant, easy to talk with and was keen to share the conversation with Rose. Rose discovered that they were related to the same person she had in mind. 'This is a new day for me, and I`m not alone anymore,. It's like a slight ray of light is shining my way and hope is finally pushing through for me,' she thought with a smile on her face. Charmaine had three sisters, Diane, Winsome and Carol, and one brother, called John, and they all lived in the same area of Kingston.

Charmaine needed a job and so Ms Peg hired her a few weeks later. Rose and Charmaine got to know each other; it was amazing the history that they shared. She worked hard and Rose could tell that she needed the job; she was put in the kitchen to wash the plates and pots. Rose had never seen anyone that took so such pride in washing crockery. The pots; she would spend so much time scrubbing them that if you had no mirror of your own, surely the pots would be perfect to use. Rose complained to Charmaine about how uncomfortable Buggy was making her life and that she wanted to leave. Charmaine felt sad for her.

" My sister Diane lives by herself, so you could come and stay with her," she said, sounding positive. Come over this weekend and we`ll talk about it." That Friday evening Rose went to see Diane, who was more than happy for her stay with her.

Rose had to make a decision soon; it was either live in Ms Peg's house and continued feeling unhappy and stressed, due to Buggy's bickering and unpleasantness, or living with this newfound relative, who she had only just met and knew nothing much about. Either way it wasn't an easy choice. She needed Pauline to understand; that was important for her and so she made every effort for that to happen. As Rose walked into the room that she shared with Pauline, she noticed that she was lying on her bed gazing up at the ceiling. Rose glanced up to see what she was looking at, But nothing was there except for a tiny spider that had been caught in its own web, – 'you don't see that every day' she thought. She decided it is now or never; she would have to make her see that it was the right thing for Rose to do by moving out. 'Oh, how I wish if I could disappear right now; how easy that would be for everyone,' she thought as she continued to gaze up at the ceiling, at the spider. Rose went and sat beside Pauline on the bed, and although she expressed herself awkwardly to Pauline, her friend listened to what she had to say.

Pauline felt her pain and did not judge her, instead she directed her anger towards her dad, whom she blamed for everything. What Rose wanted the most was to remain friends with Pauline and that would never change. They both decided that it would be a good idea for Rose, to continue working at the restaurant. Ms Peg was delighted about the decision, since she didn't have to suggested that herself. How comforting it must have felt. The day finally came when Ros, was to move out of only the home she'd known for the last six years. She packed her suitcase the night before, taking only the possessions she owned: her clothing. Since she didn't want to travel on her own to Diane`s place, she asked Diane, to come down and help her in the afternoon, after she finished work.

Rose didn't want to have to go back to the main house, the one that she had once shared as her home with Ms Peg's family, and to the room she had shared with Pauline, so she had brought her suitcase the day before and left it in one of the flats at the back of the restaurant. It was almost dark when Diane arrived. Pauline was sitting on a small chair at the back of the restaurant as she as always did. To get to the flat where Rose had her suitcase, there were two options: either you walk around by the dirt lane, or go through the restaurant. Diane wasn't going to be walked through no dirt lane. She was short, had the shape of a mermaid, her complexion was dark as coco tea without milk, and had enough confidence that say she didn't care what other people thought about her. Well, as you know Rose was from time to time very shy, but she knew who she was, and what she wanted. She didn't want to appear too bold; it would have ruined the moment, after all, everyone was watching. As Diane walked through the restaurant, she called out to Rose. Ms Peg was sitting in her little office as usual half asleep over her money drawer. Obviously, she heard the noise and the sound of movements. She opened her eyes to observe what was happening, but just sat there without saying a word. Rose could tell that she was deep in thought, but whatever it was she was thinking about one could only assume she was probably hoping that Rose would change her mind and stay, or maybe, who was going to open her restaurant in the early hours of the morning. Either way, Rose was not eager to know; the less said the better.

Rose and Diane walked past a narrow path, before they got to the flat. What should have taken two minutes felt like forever. Her nerves started kicking in, and she thought to herself, 'am I doing the right thing'? Rose, began to question herself with less contentment, as she smiled nervously. This was not the time to start having second thoughts. 'You're about to start a new life. The least you can do is to be more excited.' It was like she was talking to a second person, only she was talking to herself, in her head. Diane was already pulling the suitcase through the narrow door of the flat, into a small corridor and then down two flight of stairs that stood at the entrance of a main door. Then Rose was out and she was gone, like a captured bird, free at last. The noise the suitcase made as it rattled along was like it had its own engine attached to its raggedy ol' frame, shouting 'freedom at last, catch me if you can'.

CHAPTER 6
Moving into the SLUM

Diane walked back past Pauline, pulling the baggage without even a glance in her direction. Rose noticed that Pauline had a strange look on her face, even though she pretended not to be looking at Diane. Her face was saying something else; you could tell that she was annoyed with Diane's presence. Rose moved towards her and said,

"I'll see you in the morning Pauline".

It was clear that she felt hurt, she saw it in her eyes." Yeah, I`ll see you tomorrow, when you come into work, Rose", said Pauline, as she got up off the chair and walked into the kitchen. Knowing how sensitive Pauline could be with her feelings, Rose didn't want to say anything to make the situation any worse. It was hard enough for both of them, and so Rose hurried out the restaurant behind Diane, as fast as her weary feet could carry her. Diane took the lead, knowing that they were now arriving in her own area. They chatted on their journey; the sun was now setting in the blue skies as the birds were flying overhead in all their glory. The journey wasn't a long one, but still seemed shorter than usual. Diane seemed so excited, Rose thought she'd never seen someone so happy pulling a suitcase along. 'How strange' Rose ponder ed as she walked beside her.

There was no welcoming sign at the entrance. As they arrived in the street, Rose noticed that there were two individuals operating as vendors, selling food on the sidewalk. The man had a stove that was made from a metal drum. It appeared to have been cut in half, and four legs had been attached, so that it stood firmly to the ground. The purpose was to make a massive barbeque grill, which astonished her; it was like nothing she'd has seen before. There was smoke coming from the drum, and the fragrance of different flavours was so strong in the air, you could taste it without even having a bite. Working at Ms Peg, restaurant had no comparison to this jerky heaven. This was something very new to Rose, and it felt welcoming, homely, and she excited to see something so different from everything she had known for years. The young man was preparing chicken, and pork on the grill. He also had a small table that was laid out beside him. It was covered with plastic cloth, nicely done. He had plates, forks, napkins, and bread for his customers, he also had a pot of chicken foot soup, boiling on three large stones. This reminded Rose so much of her home, when her mother would be cooking outside, for the men on the farm, she also misses her mom and siblings dearly.

Oh, now I miss mama's cooking, she pondered, looking around, seemingly rather preoccupied. In the outside kitchen back home the fireplace also had three large stones in its bay, that kept the pot in its position. For a while Rose felt homesick, as she drifted deeper into her thoughts. Suddenly she heard a little girl, who was calling out to the woman who was working with the young man, "could you sell me one of your juices, please". Rose looked at the girl and then smiled. Business was going well at the grill, with people shouting and laughing, while buying their food. They all seemed to be familiar with each other. It wasn't barbeque chicken and pork, but jerk chicken and pork, you could hear the customers as they requested their orders. Either way it didn't matter to Rose. Just being there was enough for her, and the experience was a good one. There were also people coming home from work who were buying food. One man came to the stall looking as if he hadn't eaten for days.

"Boss man set me up good. I've been dying to get here ever since I left work. Please let me have some of the jerk chicken, and half a loaf of that fresh bread. Oh yes, a cup of that soup as well," he then paused for a moment. After much anticipation, he was given his food, he paid for the lot and then he left.

Another person came and asked, "What type of soup you got, boss?"

The man at the stall replied,

" I only got chicken foot soup today."

" OK, nice. Let me have a big cup that'll burst the gas off my stomach". After he was served, he walked towards the street, and then on towards the road where Diane lived.

Diane, too, knew the man at the jerk grill. He was captivated by her, behaving like a little love-sick puppy, that craved its owner's attention. It was obvious that she did not share his enthusiasm at all, but he didn't seem to mind. Instead, she flirted with him. Funny thing he was enjoying the ride, as if he didn't mind. He then offered her a nice juicy piece of jerk chicken, chopped up carefully and wrapped to perfection in foil paper. Some of the customers were curious as to who Rose was, and Diane was eager to explain to them that Rose was her cousin, even though they looked nothing alike, absolutely nothing. What was most interesting was the excited look she had on her face, as she continued telling them that they were related through her mother's side of the family; she explained that Diane's mother and Rose's dad were related. Everyone was saying how beautiful Rose was, and she inclined her head slightly, looking down towards the ground. 'Oh God,' she thought. All this attention is making me so uncomfortable; I wish they would just stop staring at me'. A few minutes later, Rose held her head up again to look at their faces. Some of them look transfixed by her beauty and innocence, smiling and sweating (probably from the hot spice on the jerk chicken and pork that they were indulging in). It was all a little too much and Rose signalled to Diane that she was ready to leave. She walked over to Diane and said,

"I need to go have a shower and I'm tired from my long day at work. Can we go now please"? Rose said it with a smile on her face, trying to stay in character, without sounding weird.

Diane was just finishing her conversation with one of the loudmouth customers. The woman was saying how she couldn't be bothered cooking for her kids that evening.

"I'm tired. I've been cooking every day of the week. Thank God today is Friday. I just decided that I'd come and buy some jerk chicken and pork with bread for them. I just know they'll love it for dinner. She continued with her chattering,

"Oh, by the way Martin can have some too when he gets in from work later. Rose noticed how exhausted the woman looked, and could tell by the lines on her face that although she was in her early thirties, she appeared to be much older. Maybe it was due to having so many children. Rose felt a hint of sadness towards her even though she did not know her. The dark circles under her eyes were evidence of her lack of sleep, reminding Rose, of when her mother had a breakdown. Diane glanced up at Rose and gestured that she was ready to go,

"See you later," she said to the woman, as she walked off pulling the suitcase behind her. As they walked further up the street, Rose noticed that the left side of the street had a huge wall, as if it were there protecting something sacred. What was obvious to her was that most of

98

the houses also had a wall around their perimeter but were of a shorter design. The houses were visible, it was more like fences or gates, if you like. Further up the street the design of the houses began to change; they were now looking much smaller and built from wooden structures.

Diane went through a zinc gate just wide enough to allow two people to walk through at once. To Rose's astonishment it was a big yard with about six houses crowded there close together. Her eyes widened as she saw how close the houses were to each other. 'Oh my God, she thought to herself, 'this is something I would not have imagined'. There were two paths that led to Diane's house; walking to Charmaine's place was one way to get there;. That entrance would avoid seeing most of the people and houses in the yard. Rose never did use the other way – the main gate – because she always wanted to stop by Charmaine`s first.

It was like a story book, where the neighbours would be talking to each other through their windows, passing through whatever they must give or borrow. There were people sitting on their doorsteps, chatting and laughing as if it were their daily activity; you could tell it was a normal thing for them, while others were moving around like ghosts in a graveyard, having nothing to do but swirl around like leaves in the wind.

Diane said hello to everyone that she saw in the yard, and they all seemed very interested in Rose, who had no intention of standing there with them as she was too tired for chit chatting but she just kept smiling. She was good at hiding her emotions, and wasn't about to show fear. Rose believed that people think you're weak if you show fear, and that was not going to happen.

" Diane, who is this lady?" one woman asked, inquisitively.

"My cousin," she replied, "but she is tired now. I'll see you later".

When they walked off Rose said to her softly and looking even more exhausted,

"Not me. I won't be coming back out tonight."

"That's OK cuz," I only told her that so we could leave".

They would often call her cuz, which was short for cousin after that, as if it made them feel more connected to her, but she didn't mind the name calling. At least people would stop asking the same questions whenever they saw them together; some of them so close in your face, you could smell what they had for lunch and Rose did not like it.

Diane lived in a small one-bedroom wooden house; it had an area that she used for her kitchen, which was nothing like Rose had ever seen before. All the houses in the yard were almost the same in size, but there was one that that stood out from the others right in the middle of the yard, like a proud peacock. It was much larger, and had three bedrooms. It looked old enough, that it might have been there for years. Rose contemplated that this must belong to the owner, but did not ask any questions. Rose was eager to have a shower and so Diane went next door and asked her friend for the bathroom key. They were literally living three metres apart from each other. The only thing that kept them separated, was a tiny flowers garden that had beautiful roses in it. Rose observed a small wooden hut; she thought it was probably a toilet but later learnt it was someone's home. She asked Diane about it and was shocked to hear that someone actually lived there. She didn't know what to say. She bit her nails as she struggled to think how to respond to that, but in the end all she said was,

"Is this a bad joke."

Diane laughed as she placed her hands on her hips

"Oh, who is living their?" Rose asked curiously.

"A woman and her son" Diane, answered.

"Honestly, I don't know what to say! Is she OK?" she asked, feeling uneasy.

" It's just the way it is cuz a lot of people that live here are poor like me, but we manage to survive," she said with a hint of sadness in her voice.

Rose sighed.

"Let me get the key from my friend, so you can have your shower cuz it`s getting late."

A tall chocolate coloured woman came to the door. She looked to be in her late twenties. She had a set of keys in one hand, staring down on Rose. She said hello to Diane, then asked,

"Is this your cousin that you were talking about?" and when Diane concurred she turned to Rose and said with a smile on her face,

"Nice to meet you, Rose,". Rose nodded her head politely and said to her,

"How are you? Nice to meet you, too." s

She then introduced herself as Dauta.

"Oh that's quite a name," Rose said to her, jokingly. "I like your sense of humour."

The woman excused herself, saying that she had to go and make a cup of milo tea for my son before he went to bed, but that she hoped to see Rose again tomorrow. She gave Diane the keys she held in her hand and went back inside her house. It looked like a it was a two bedroom house and you could tell that it was newly built. Diane walked towards the bathroom and opened it. It had one single shower that was built on the wall, and Rose noticed that there were small holes in the wall which she wasn't too pleased about. She thought to herself, 'well, since its night, I`ll take my chances, but hell no, I won't be having a shower during the daytime' and with that she hurried to finish her shower and get out. It was the awareness of feeling exposed that Rose felt uncomfortable with.,

" Diane, how can you take showers in that place?" she asked.

"Did something happen ? "Diane asked, with a puzzled look on her face, so Rose explained what she had observed.

There was also an outside flush toilet that was just big enough to fit only one person inside, and the bathroom was so close to it that you'd probably think they were joined. It was obvious that most of the tenants shared the same facilities, and Rose worried that she was going to find it awkward, knowing that she wasn't used to being in such confined spaces. Living in one house and sharing the same facilities, was hard enough with people that you aren't related to, like at Ms Pe's, house. Imagine having an urgency to use the toilet or bathroom, and someone decided to rush in just before you did, or even worse forming a line like school children. Rose thought of different scenarios and how things would play out, especially now that she realised she would be sharing with God knew, how many people. This was going to be challenging; it was like being forced to eat mud with a smile on your face. After Rose had her shower, she went inside the wooden one room house. It was almost nine thirty at night, and she had work the following day, so her only concern was getting some sleep. The chatting and laugher outside was so loud, including Diane`s contribution to the hubbub when she returned the keys to her friend, Dauta .

Rose was out cold as soon as her head hit the pillow, but before she slept, she prayed to God, asking for his protection for the people that she cared for, including herself. Her eyes were wandering through the tiny cracks of the wooden house, and could see the light flickering outside, in the back of the yard. Was that the shadows of tree branches? Or maybe it was person standing there. She hoped if it was, that they wouldn't come in. She glanced at the clock when she heard Diane come back into the house and saw it was about twelve thirty. Rose wasn't a sound sleeper and was always aware of her surroundings. She thought that might be her way of sleeping in such a way that protected her. It was almost morning, and Rose was awake, but just lay there in bed, thinking about what her day was going be like, working at the restaurant. The feeling was overwhelming, almost too much to bear, 'How will I survive? God have mercy upon me,' she thought in despair. She shuffled out of bed, feeling a little less tired than the day before, but then she realised it was psychological, all the worry was in her own head. Rose got dressed and was ready to leave for work; it was seven in the morning and that would be normal when she had been living at Ms Peg`s, but she decided that getting there at seven thirty, like the other employers should be fine. For the first time in a long while Rose was taking control of her life and she felt liberated.

Diane was already awake when Rose was ready to leave,.

"Hey cuz, stop looking so worried, it will be OK. If it gets too much, just come back home", she reassured Rose.

"Thanks. I'll see you later. Don't want to be late on my first day back," Rose said to Diane, as she stepped out into her new world of freedom. Most of the residents that lived in the yard were still sleeping in their beds, as she went through the main zinc gate, although a few early birds were already up embracing the sidewalk with their asses. Rose went by, feeling awkward. She was surprised to see so many people sitting out so early. You'd probably think they had duties to perform in their houses. She was never one to wear a frown, so she put on a brave face and said good morning to everyone she saw, and the women answered her politely. There was one woman who was paying close attention to Rose. 'Why is she acting so odd,' Rose pondered. The woman kept rubbing her nose, as if her brain was going to fall out.

"So, you're going to work early?" she said. Sounding off key "Yes," Rose replied. I try to be on time most of the time. What time will you be going to your job?" Rose asked the woman, assuming she had one.

"I`m not working, just now," the woman said. Lost it about a month ago

"Oh sorry to hear that. It's OK," she stuttered, appearing to be embarrassed.

They were officially the village gossiping champions. She could see that they didn't want to be missing out on anything. Rose felt her stomach tightening with uneasiness. 'This is a productive practice; what can they possible gain?' Rose, asked herself. She felt their eyes piercing through her body, like incursive photography, snaping away without permission – more like having a body scan done. She felt like she'd had her entire being examined as she walked off down the street. Diane didn't have a regular job. She used to work in a garment factory called the Free Zone, was managed by Chinese immigrants, who had migrated to Jamaica. They manufactured T shirts and panties that were then shipped off to different countries around the world, included America. It was the best option for most of them to get a job, especially if you were uneducated and needed employment. For the most part it made the women feel independent, and value their self-worth, even though it was low paid; it put food on their tables.

To them it meant everything; to them, helping their families was more important than anything. Rose later learnt that a lot of the women that lived in the area were once employees of Free Zone, and had suffered a great loss when unfortunately, the company went into liquidation. They all lost their jobs, leaving some with absolutely nothing. Rose now understood more about their lackadaisical behaviour. For most of the women, they couldn't find jobs easily, due to lack of skills and educational background; the men were more able to achieve that. It was easier for them to find jobs in supermarkets, moving, and handling heavy packages, driving delivery trucks, bus conductors, getting odd jobs here and there, whatever they were able to find to support their families. The women would stay at home and look after the children. There were a few that were vendors, selling what was available. Some got jobs working as domestic helpers; jobs which paid peanuts, but they didn't complain.

Diane was a survivor; she was never a person to sit around and wait for a man to take care of her. She was a small vendor during the school period, and would buy whatever was in demand, and sell it to the school children. During the school holidays Diane would buy bread fruit, and ackee juice and open her stall at the bottom of the street. It was impossible for her to attain a big profit from her sales; sometimes it was just enough to buy food, and stock to continue selling. She could have taken the easy route out, like many of the other girls did, but instead she wanted to be free, independent. She had good morals, and Rose was impressed with her qualities; that was something special. Even though she was poor, she often said that no one would hire her, due to the area that she lived in. It was sad though, how society judges individuals from their background and where they live. Rose believed that most of those people were victims of that system. Some people had fell victim of their environment, while others found a purpose to motivate themselves, accomplishing something. No matter how insignificant others might think or believe her to be, Diane was one of them.

Charmaine dated one of the guys who worked for Ms Peg. Rose didn't like him much, he was loudmouthed, rude and controlling. He was tall and slender and his body was cover with scars as if he had been in an accident. You could tell he was a coward; the only strength he had was bullying women. Rose didn't understand what Charmaine saw in him; she deserved so much better, but it was her choice who she chose to date. Rose got to know Charmaine's other siblings. They were all welcoming, friendly, and kind and looked out for each other. When Rose met them, there was the sisters, Carol and Diane, and they had one brother called Ackee Belly. That was quite an unusual name. 'What was his mother thinking?' Rose thought, as she smiled at him. She later learnt that wasn't his real. That was the given to him by his friends because of his exceptional love for the fruit; even when they were only half ripe he would pick and cook them. Winsome was one of Charmaine's sisters who came along and resided there. They lived in the same area of Kingston, practically neighbours and saw each other every day. How awesome was that, or maybe not? It was amazing to see the bond they shared, even thought they had their differences, but what family doesn't? Their togetherness was way greater.

The journey to the restaurant only took Rose a few minutes; you could see it when standing at the bottom of the road. When Rose got there that first morning, Ms Peg was already at the restaurant, and was preparing the breakfast in the kitchen. Rose felt uneasy, her heart was beating faster, but she had no intention of letting anyone seeing that. Instead, she walked in bravely, and said,

"Good morning".

Ms Peg's expression was one of relief when she saw it was Rose.

"Good morning, Rose", she called back. "Are you ok?"

"Yes, I'm doing good, thank you," she responded putting on a brave face. Ms Peg had one of those faces that could not hide emotions. Rose believed she was her own worst enemy, but this time her face was showing genuine care towards Rose, and she didn't see that very often. Rose had her own little nickname for Ms Peg. Whenever she would irritate Rose, she would think of her as a stone- faced ornament that doesn't speak, but just stood in one place and stared without blinking. She would then pretend you were invisible, ignoring your very existence.

Anyway, she washed her hands and went into the kitchen to help. She felt strange wasn't sure of what to do; make small talk, or just keep quiet. While she was there pondering as to what to do, Ms Peg, broke the silence with an apology for what had happened. Looking at her, Rose wasn't sure what to say, but eventually she told her that it was alright; she shouldn't blame herself. A part of Rose felt sorry for her, knowing that she, too, was a victim and that there was nothing she could have done. 'Well,' she thought, 'I need to act with more confidence in myself. That's the only way I'm going to survive the day, and many more days to come.' A few of the other employers came into work about eight, while others were late; bad timekeepers who couldn't be on time to save their lives.

Pauline came in during the serving of breakfast. She was delighted to see Rose, and was glowing as if it was Christmas, smiling as she walked towards Rose, greeting her with,

"Big head morning?"

They had a strange way of greeting each other, and Rose found her remarks hilarious.

"Oh, whatever big eyes," She quipped in reply, just as if nothing had happened. In fact nothing had happened, at least not between them. If anything their friendship had become stronger. The day went well, and later in the afternoon when Pauline and Rose were relaxing together, out of nowhere Pauline said to Rose wearing a half frowned and her face,

"I don't like Diane".

"Why? I was wondering when you would mention that," Rose replied. She didn't want to discuss Diane, but Pauline was her friend, before she ever met Diane. With the blood pumping through her veins, she felt her body building up into a temperature, as she tried to sound reasonable. The sweat that settled on her forehead, was now dripping into her eyes. Rose looked at Pauline and said,

"Let me get some napkins to wipe my face. It really is hot today.

"You're avoiding the topic!"

"No I'm not. Honestly, I'm not," Rose denied the accusation vehemently.

"That's OK then. Go get your napkin and come straight back."

Rose walked off to get the napkin and then she returned.

"There! You see, I'm not avoiding you, Pauline," she said with a smile on her face.

They were always very truthful with each other, never showing unkindness when communicating about their feelings; respect was always important to their friendship. That was one of the reasons, they got on so well. Rose, sat beside her on an ol' wooden stool and said to her,

"So, why are you being such a hater?"

"Well for starters, she's acting as if she knew you before I did. She's so short and rude, can imagine if she was taller". Rose didn't like where the conversation was leading to.

"Come on now. Is this necessary. All this silly name calling! You're better than that; at least I thought you were."

Pauline looked a little embarrassed because of what Rose thought of her.

"I do understand," she continued, "as to why you might be feeling that way, but she is a good person."

"I don't hate her," she said picking at her fingernails, as if she was going to pull them out. I`m not judging. You're my friend. Nothing or no one can change that; moving on doesn't change anything."

"I know," Pauline said, pushing back her hair out of her face; she had thick hair that was down past her shoulders; it was always well kept, and had bright golden highlights that made her stand out in a crowd. Rose had always admired that about her.

They spoke for a while until they started to reminisce about the years that had gone by, and how life was much simpler then. Rose, burst out laughing,

"What are you talking about girl, you've always had an easy life"."

"I know it's been harder for you, Rose, in every way. What I meant was that we're getting older, and things won't always stay the same.

"Yes. Don't you think I know that? But when that day comes, we will be ready. All that I 've been through, it will help me to be a stronger person. I will not make this ruin my life; I will fight until the day I die. I want you to promise me that you, too, will be strong when your journey begins."

Pauline was so impressed with Rose`s words.

"When did you became so wise?

"I'm not really, but when life comes at you hard, after a while you must learn how to cope; otherwise it will consume you.

The sun was setting behind the clouds, and the birds were flying higher into the air to get home. It was time for Rose to go, and so she said her goodbyes. Ms Peg was half asleep over her money drawer as usual, but managed to open her eyes as Ros, went past into the kitchen to share some food. Pauline was walking behind her.

"Share it for me, please?" Pauline said as she handed her the food box.

Rose did always prefer i, when Pauline shared her food. She would often fill the box with chicken and whatever else was available. Ms Peg was sweating in that tiny office, and she got up and went outside. She sat around the back-entrance door on an old chair that seemed to have been there forever. How she managed that heat was a mystery. It was cooler outside; the fresh air was so energising and you could tell that she was enjoying it. There were a lot of people in the street as Rose walked home; some people were standing in groups, talking and laughing with each other. Rose was not familiar with most of the streets that ran off the main road, and some of the stories she had heard about the gangs would scare the daylight out of her. The streets were really close together; everyone was practically neighbours, so it didn't make sense to Rose why they often became rivals and fought against each other.

There was this tyre shop that Rose had to walk pass every evening, when going home. Some of the guys who worked there would often say hello to her, with the intention of catching her attention, but she wasn't interested. Instead, she just smiled; to be polite was the right thing to do, and Rose knew it was important to keep herself safe. If they disliked you for whatever reason, your life would be a living hell. Pretending had become a way of existence for Rose; she really wished she could tell them to go away, but she understood that this was better. It was always the same thing every day; people would be sitting on the sidewalk, chatting and laughing or gossiping. This was becoming too frequent, one would perhaps think, they had no home and were living on the sidewalk. The worse part was the staring. It left a bad taste in her mouth, she felt their eyes were striping her down, non-stop until she was out of sight. Rose wished she did not have to see them so constantly. 'I'd rather work on a plantation than put up with this every day' she thought to herself, feeling annoyed.

Occasionally she would find the neighbours or friends arguing; the language that they used would burn your ear off, it was so fierce and intense. At times she thought they were going to get physical with each other, but that was never the case for them. Rose thanked God for that as she could not bear the thought of what would happen. Rose often talked to herself and no one could hear her except for herself; people would probably believe that she was losing her mind if they knew. It was like meditation, connecting to one's inner self was a good way of putting things into perspective, without any interference. Expressing herself was not the easiest thing for her; Rose had difficulties trusting people. Well, she made a promise to herself, that she would not be like her fellow acquaintances, even though obviously, she was living among them.

Living in Kingston had its ups and downs, and there were times when running away would be your best alternative due to the level of criminal activity that was taking place there. Rose was often frightened and could feel her heartbeat quickening inside her chest. The gun shots would echo in the distance; sometimes closer than you could imagine. Listening, you might hear some unfortunate poor soul running off into the wrong direction, followed by horrifying screams. It's obvious what has happened – a murder; families were burying their loved ones too often. Most of the time there was no real reason, it was just too easy to kill another person, showing no regard or empathy for what they did. It was best to be an amiable person, getting on with everyone. It allowed you to connect better. Rose found it tough processing everything, living in the place, adapting to the lifestyle. Where she lived had a comparatively low crime rate, and was also the smallest district around the area; most of the men were law abiding citizens, just trying to get by, going to work and supporting their families.

The surrounding areas were off the charts, with impoverishment on the rise, and a lack of medical care plus youths murdering each other. Nothing felt normal except she was still breathing. Deep down Rose knew that one day she would leave. She sat on the steps, near the front door entrance. At Diane's house it was early evening; she had a book in her hands, reading, when suddenly she heard a sound that she become all too familiar with. Screams of another life gone, but this time it was too close for comfort. The only thing that kept the communities apart was a zinc fence.

"Oh my god," she cried, as the book fell from her grip. She quickly got up and went inside, securing herself under the bed. Rose heard the sound of feet running towards the board house, ripping through the zinc like a wild boar hunting for its prey. There were mobsters passing through. She felt her bones rattling, like a train on a railroad track. She listened intently, holding her nerves together with every breath in her body. Realisation came that they weren't stopping and Rose whispered, "Thank you, Father God". It was their regular escape route; everyone was scared but didn't dare to say it. Rose finally ascertains that was their way, it was a problematic situation; and she would surely have to adjust to it.

Rose learnt the art of survival Getting on with the village folk was important to her, even those who were not so worthy. To accomplish this she, had to master her fear to acquire the abilities to progress. Believing in what she hoped to gain, was the only way to get there. It was her mission to remain true to herself, while at the same time, been part of the community; accruing few goods friends after a while had made life less difficult. she found she could do this but was still able to stay in her element. Nadine lived a few metres across the street from Rose. She appeared to be quiet, friendly and they had something in common – their belief that one day, things would change, when the right opportunity came along, and they would leave the community to get to a better place. At first Nadine would just say hello to Rose, whenever they saw each other, often making small conversation. Eventually they became friends. She showed signs of insecurity, and was always worried what others thought of her. She had two young sons at the time, and the youngest had a disability, which was challenging for him. He was a good kid. Nadine did her best to keep him safe. Occasionally he would hurt himself, or be hurt by the other children. The system had no special requirements in place for assisting children like him.

The residents who lived in that area, regardless of their differences, were kind and caring towards each other. But, always they would be complaining about the problems they were going through to anyone who was willing to listen. Everyone had a pattern that reflected their personality. They were aware of their positions; considering their lives, that wasn't so hard to accomplish. The gossipers, news-carriers, a few troubles makers, the list would go on and on, but that was their way.

For some life had proven harder than for others. but for all, providing the everyday essentials was difficult for them. Feeding their children was a burden; they faced struggles whichever way they turned. They would borrow money so that their children could be fed, hiding their disappointment – no parents would want their children to see that. Some of the women would still be having babies, even though they couldn't afford, the ones they already had. It was heart-breaking to see. Probably by staying home and having more children they thought they would be secure enough. But still they would be abandoned by the men, that who did not see the need in marrying them, apprehensive of commitment. As humiliating as it seems, it was a conventional practice. Rose was a keen observer; she could have been a great detective, but that was not her calling; people's issues were their own affair. She was having her own moment, speaking with her inner self; it was what she knew best. Why these women believed themselves so insignificant was a scandal – it was shameful. It was like they had given up all hope of anything better for themselves.

Rose's parents did not have much, but nothing compared to what some of these people were going through. It was the first time she had witnessed such poverty and deprivation. Where she came from there were a few people living in poverty, but this was a wider scale beyond her comprehension. A family of four would be living in just a one room, sharing the same space with only the partition of a curtain that rans across the room separating them. Day in and say out, they had the same expression on their faces. Rose saw their tired raggedy bodies, walking back and forth, as if the weight of the world was on their shoulders. Some looked like zombies, transitioning, lost in oblivion; wondering what tomorrow might bring for them and their families. The women were having baby after baby; it was disheartening to see, but Rose felt more sympathy for the children. But through their time of trouble and hardship, they were still able to show kindness towards each other. It was a beautiful thing to witness, even more rewarding to know they were still human. There were days when a few families couldn't even provide, for their children or have money to send them to school. However, asking a close friend for some food was a normal enough thing for them to do.

Everyone knew each other's business; it was like one big family without secrets, like living in a goldfish bowl. Rose saw all this but she was determined she wasn't going to give in and become like them. One day, Rose decided that she needed to go through the large zinc gate, to get a feel of their outside world. Some of the women were sitting on the sidewalk, laughing, and talking as usual. They seemed quite comfortable around each other. As Rose entered through the gate all eyes were traveling in her direction. It was like crossing a road without thinking. You might be hit by a car, but you did it anyway because you weren't sure of what to do, that was how she felt.

It had taken a while for Rose to settle into her new home with Diane, and adjust to her new life in this underprivileged community, but eventually Rose decided that it was time that she went back to nursing school. It has been a while, settling with Dian, and adjusting into a community that were so underdeveloped it was a lot to deal with. However, the once untroubled area that Rose had previously walked through to attend her classes had now became a battle ground for a turf war. She was determined to resume her studies but to even find a new route was proving to be exhausting; it was almost impossible to

115

achieve that goal. She had to travel twice the journey, spending money and bus fare that she did not really have. But her worst fear of all was that what had happened previously would occur again, and she wasn't ready to be traumatized by bandits again. The evenings were getting too dark, and Rose was not up for any unpleasant encounters; she did not think she could survive another. It made her shiver in fear.

Diane was barely making enough money on her stall to buy stock, or even food. And for some reason she could not get a regular job; maybe working for herself was more fulfilling. Rose had a steady income every week, from working at Ms Peg restaurant, and with that she was able give more money to Diane towards food; she was willing to help, after all it was the right thing to do.

A few months after Rose went back to nursing school, the teacher who taught her so brilliantly went to bed one night and died in her sleep. Rose was heartbroken, she did not know what to do, as unfortunately, there was no other teacher to replace the poor woman. This was bad.

"Why me lord? Not again. At least you could have showed me a sign. That was my savings, all I had. I am sorry about thinking about my own loss, instead of the family of the deceased. But why?" she prayed.

There wasn't much that Rose could have done, and in the end she had to move on. Diane and the others were very supportive of her. Rose thought that some things in life are not meant to be, or maybe it just wasn't her time.

Where Rose was residing with Diane, it was good enough for its purpose and she was forever grateful. At times, Diane's boyfriend would stay over. It was an awkward arrangement for everyone to be sleeping in the same bedroom, but Diane got things under control; the bed originally had two mattresses to its four-legged frame. She took one off, placing it upon the kitchen floor. Rose was given the honour of sleeping on the bed. Diane, tried to explain as best as she could how uncomfortable situation was to her; she thought the world of Rose, and did not want to lose that respect. To be honest it felt strange at first, but she had to remembered it was Diane`s home, not hers. So, whatever she was feeling had no relevance to the matter. Nevertheless, Rose felt like family, and didn't want to upset anyone, and in time she learned to adopt, and adjust to her conditions without whining.

]

Chapter 7

THE UNDISCOVER SONGBIRD

Rose had always loved to sing, but after the unexpected event when her nursing tutor died, she realised that it was time to move on with what was left of her entangled life. She acknowledges that having a job was still a good thing. She thought to herself, 'I am never going to leave this place', as she bowed her head down on her knees. Pauline had a friend, and his brother was a popular reggae artist at the time. He would come around sometimes, to visit her, so she told him about how talented Rose, was. Pauline's friend told his brother, of Rose's talent, and eventually he came around to meet her. He came across as being interested about her singing abilities and writing habits. He thought she had a great voice. Rose was excited that maybe, after all she could possible, make it in having a singing career. She could finally be able to take care of her siblings, and mother as she always wanted to do. In the next couple of weeks Rose started going to the studios with Bolo, hoping that she would record her first song.

They decided on a song; it was a famous cover, originally recorded by an American artist. Another popular artist had previously done a cover the year before, so Bolo thought it would be good having, a female singer doing a cover version. She was working really hard in the studio day after day. Rose's version sounded amazing; she would spend hours in the studio rehearsing, and she felt hopeful that she might finally be able to assist Jena and Del, her youngest siblings, to get a better education. She deliberated to herself about how proud her family would be about her being a singer. 'Oh, I could take mama away from everything,' she thought as she sat there daydreaming. Rose was delighted about the future; it took her mind off all the disappointment she had when she wasn't able to complete her nursing course. She was a deeply wounded each time she was knocked down, but Rose would always return with something different.

Rose was visiting Maria, more often than before, and when she told her about her plan she was very excited for her. Everything was in place for recording tracks of her cover song to be released.

"Oh my, Rose! This is amazing! Your voice sounds great," Maria told her after listening to the cassette that Rose played for her. Everyone in the house was dancing with so much happiness, Rose felt overjoyed.

"Well, Bola said that the record will be released in a few weeks," Rose told her sister.

"Really," Maria replied.

"Yes, he's on tour now, in Europe, so I'm hoping it will come through when he returns," she explained, and then she started singing the song again. The weekend was over, and the next day it was time for Rose to return to Kingston. She got up early to catch the bus, it drove through different areas until finally they arrived in downtown Kingston. Rose had to catch another bus to her destination, but first to had to go home before going to work. She called Ms Peg, to inform her that she wasn't able to come in that day, as she wasn't feeling very well. She could imagine the expression on Ms Peg's face , she thought to herself.

"Ok Rose," the woman replied. "I was hoping you'd be able to come in today." She cleared her throat as if something was stuck in it, then continued, "Because we're really shorthanded as Jeff didn't come in today." She sighed! "And it's a little busy right now." It was hard listening to the disappointment in her voice as if Rose, was the owner, and she was left in charge. Rose felt burdened by her sudden urge.

" Oh well! Sorry. I wish I could come in, but it's just that, I'm not feeling well, Ms Peg", said Rose, sounding poorly over the phone, coughing, as if she needed to lie down. "I`ll see how tomorrow goes, Ms Peg. I', no good to anyone like this. Bye", she said as she hung up the phone. 'What is that woman playing at? She`s acting as if am supposed to be feeling guilty,' Rose thought to herself.

Diane disrupted her thoughts by saying,

" what did she say?"

"Who?" Rose asked her.

"You're looking upset."

"No, not really". It's just that even though I told Ms Peg that I wasn't well, she basically wouldn't have minded if I went in to work."

"Really," Diane said, rolling her eyes, what does she take you for?

"I don't know how you work with that woman."

"She's not that bad you know," Rose tried to defend her. "I know she's just odd, but anyway, I need my job". She nodded her head, "people like those you must find a borderline to be around them. Honestly I'm not worried," she said looking at Diane with a whacky smile.

"Diane, tomorrow is a new dawn," Rose said excitedly.

"Hmm?" she said, looking confused as if she didn't know what Rose was referring to.

Rose burst out with laugher; do you even know what I'm talking about?"

"No, not really. Fill me in."

"I was talking about my song."

"Oh yeah! Cuz that song is quite good. Everyone that heard it believes you're talented."

She wasn't going to get overly excited, but was glad they thought that about her. She then reminded herself how happy she had been doing her nursing, but then see what happened! Rose cleared her throat ,looking disappointed.

"Fine, but I'm thinking this time it'll be different,

"Why?" Rose asked but could see that Diane was searching for the right thing to say. Suddenly she stood up and said, I believe in you too cuz . Don't let paste mishaps take away your joy.

"Yeah, I guess you're right. It's just that it wasn't a good feeling, but life is a lesson to be learnt. "

Rose felt a sense of caring coming from Diane, She smiled at her, then replied, "Thanks for the advice, that was nice of you. When Bola returns, my song should be released, I'm hoping he hadn't been joking around, because some of those entertainers, you know, just play around with people's lives."

"You're still going on about that, cuz?"

"No not really, just saying." Rose, got up from the step, and went inside the house, feeling frustrated. "What a contradiction Diane's remarks had been. She changed the subject of the conversation hastily, by asking Diane,

"What are you cooking for dinner, today? ,"You know it's your turn to cook."

"Yeah," she replied, half smiling. "It's chicken-back and white rice."

"Sound good to me," Rose responded, lowering her tone. She continued by saying, "please don't buy the mega pieces. They're too bony."

Diane didn't respond but turned away, laughing.

Rose wasn't ready to give up on her musical dreams, even though she'd never had a real break,; just a lifetime of memories. It was difficult for female artists to get to the top without been mistreated, especially if they had no one powerful or famous in your corner. To even get them to recognise your existence was a relentless ordeal. Eventually some women would literally become a prostitute, sleeping with every man who promised them salvation. Just maybe if you were lucky enough to get a break, it might be short lived, leaving you with no source of income, and then ultimately you won't be remembered. Except the girls who slept around with every Tom, Dick, and Harry, of course. They'd be branded and tossed in the trash. Rose heard the stories but was determined, not to suffer a similar fate. She once had a close encounter, but wasn't as gullible as people thought her to be. She saw the signs. Rose felt scared but refused to show any weakness, her morals were important to her, something she couldn't throw away so easily. She enjoyed singing, she told Pauline one day as they sat talking. She explained how hard it was for a woman, and that it was really savage out there.

"Did something happen?" Pauline asked.

"Hmm! No and I won't allow such misconduct," she replied. Poor Rose. She had no one to fight in her corner. "It`s draining my energy."

"Are you giving up, Rose?" her friend asked, looking at her with compassion.

Rose sighed! "No! I`m just waiting on Bola to come back"

A few weeks had passed and Pauline informed Rose that Bola had returned.

"Oh really! When did he get back?" she asked?

"About two days ago, his brother told me," She replied.

"Hope he doesn't procrastinate with my song, because it's been a while now that I've been waiting on him."

Looking concerned, Pauline, said

"I hope so, too, because I don't like his movements.

Rose sat and a chair observing Pauline`s face.

"Why did you say? Has something happened? she asked Pauline.

"It's just that he's been back about a week now.",

"What?" I thought you said it was two days ago. Rose was silent for a while, then she said,

"But why did you lie?" Sounding defeated, she continued, "sorry I felt so bad when I heard that"

" I wanted to protect you,"; her friend blurted out.

Rose, could see how miserable Pauline was.

" It's OK. It's not your fault. I should have known better than to trust him, but I thought he might be different"."

"Wait until we see him, maybe we`re jumping to conclusions", Pauline said, trying to console her friend.

Rose hissed through her teeth and rolled her eyes

"My gut is telling that it won't make any difference It's just a matter of time," she said, walking towards the kitchen feeling agitated. "So when are you going to see his brother again?"

"Hopefully tomorrow." Was the reply. "I`ll speak to his brother, if he turns up yeah".

" I just want to give him a message to deliver to that ol' trickster".

A few days after, Bola came by the restaurant to see Rose.

"Yes, my singer," he greeted her.

"Hello she said," as she gazed at him, as he continued to speak. "Things are in progress right now."

"Really! And if your brother didn't give you my message, you wouldn't be here, would you? Rose responded.

"Don't say that, my sister. I was coming to see you before my brother gave me your message." Rose looked at him closely, as if she was trying to read his mind, then she said, "we`ll see if you're a man of your words."

She was feeling sceptical about the whole thing, but even so hoping for the best, was all that she could do. Bola reassured Rose that he would come through and her song would be released within two weeks. He then left and went on his way; she called out to Pauline, who was standing close by. "Do you believe him?" she asked.

"He seems sure of what he was saying. Let`s wait and see."

She could tell that Pauline was trying to stay positive for her sake.

" Hey, no need to be so tense," Rose said, smiling at her friend.

But three weeks passed by since she saw Bola, and nothing seemed to be happening. Just another broken dream came crashing down on her. Rose was devastated. She heard nothing from him but somehow she wasn't surprised, as if she always knew that his words meant nothing. She would often sit by herself, lamenting about what she could have achieved as a recording artist. Now that dream was drifting further away, like a ship cast upon the ocean without a sail, not certain of where the journey was going to take her.

So It was just one more devastating moment for Rose, something that she wasn't a stranger to anymore. In fact, she now believed that this was to become a permanent place for her, in a world she despised. The weeks became months, and still Rose heard nothing, from that backstabbing liar Bola, who made a promise that he had no intention of seeing through. 'I hope he rots in hell' she thought; no one bothers to be honest about anything, lying is much easier; what a world we're living in. Pauline was always there for Rose, and now she needed her more than ever. They would sit down and talk for hours trying to make sense of it all. Even though she was living at Diane's place, it was early days to be leaning on her for such devoted support. In the end Rose had a choice to make; either she was going to swim or drown; so much disappointment, but it wasn't the end of the world. Some days were better than others, but Rose was determined not to wallow in self-pity. 'I've been through worse, this isn't the time to give in' she kept telling herself. Rose was very accustomed to talking to herself, and often would speak aloud unaware of her surroundings, which might lead some people to think that she was losing her mind. Pauline heard her a few times and gave her an odd look.

" I'm not going insane," Rose said, defending herself, when she saw the way Pauline was looking at her.

"Sorry Rose didn't mean to stare. I was coming through the door when I heard you talking, and I thought you were speaking to someone, but clearly you're not.

"It's just that I'm concerned about you.

"Rest assured I'm OK, it's just a habit I developed. It helps me to settle whenever making decisions. Who was she trying to fool, deep down Rose, felt so broken and worthless because no matter what she did, no matter how hard she tried, nothing ever seemed to work.

"OK. I understand, but next time could you not speak so loudly? It's really confusing, imagine if it was someone else standing here. What would have happened then? People only need to hear you just the once, talking to yourself. It'd soon be spreading like wildfire, so please be careful ," she warned her calmly. Rose started crying,

"I know it's not easy but I'm doing my best, honestly. I'm fine."

She then dried her face and said, "Yes, how can I go wrong when you're here. "

Pauline smiled, "We're like sisters, that's what we are. "If the wheel should turn, you would do the same for me, wouldn't you?

"Yes, within a heartbeat," Rose said cheerfully, "but from now on you'll see the new and improved me."

Pauline responded with ,"You don't have to impress me. I've come to my own conclusions and I don't want you to throw in the towel in just yet.

"What do you think?" Rose asked her friend, Pauline.

"If that's what you want to do, I'll support you. Just don't shut me out. It would be nice to see you out there one day, my singer friend" she stated.

As time went by Rose, was back to her old self, smiling, joking just being her own amusing character, but there was something different about her too. She was fierce, bolder, smarter and no one would cause any more unwelcome embarrassment to her now. Rose studied the signs, and was always ready with her defence. Rose believed that people will put you under a disadvantage, when they see you as vulnerable. But deep down she was still the same Rose underneath. To the outside world, she wanted to appear to be in control and that's what she did.

One day a man called Travis came to the restaurant where Rose worked. He seemed to be spiritual in some way, and was wearing a strange cap on his head. At first Rose thought that probably he was a monk, but surely they didn't get monks like that in Jamaica? Perhaps they did, and she wasn't aware or maybe he was a holy man in his own rights. It kept going on and on in her head. Travis and Rose met through a mutual friend who knew them both. Garvin was a musician and played for a band. Occasionally he would invite Rose to perform with them at some small event. However, it wasn't a long-term thing, and the band went their separate ways. Rose and Garvin kept in touch for some time. Garvin told Travis about Rose and so he was eager to meet her. Travis told Rose that he had tried pursuing, a career as a solo artist but didn't go far. Because of his love for music, he had been performing in bands ever since then. He went on to say that he needed a second female singer for his group and that she was recommended by a trusted friend. He did know some popular reggae artists that were in the business, but Rose remained hesitant. she was reluctant to take him up on his offer as it required travelling, sometimes, at weekends to different locations performing. Rose asked Pauline what she thought about the idea. Of course, Pauline thought it would be a new beginning for Rose, but stressed that it was her choice, it was totally up to her whether or not to take up the offer.

"I need to find out more about him, too," Rose reflected. "Maybe he's a serial killer" she said with a straight face." He did mention Garvin's name, otherwise he wouldn't have found her. In fact, she didn't know him.

"Oh my god, you're serious," Pauline laughed.

"Yes, I am. No one will ever take me for a fool again. He looks noble and respectable, but let's see what happens. He could be anything for all we know, and worse, he's not from around here. Travis was determined that Rose should believe in his project and that he was for real.

"Why are you so suspicious of me?" he asked her. gazing at her as if his mind was going into fast forward. "I could call Garvin, if you think that I'm not for real". "No said Rose, I will talk with him soon."

"If you'd been through what I have, you wouldn't trust you either" was her heartfelt response. "Was it that bad," he asked, trying to wrap his head around what she was saying. "Yes, it was but I don't want to talk about it, OK?"

"That's fine. I understand," he said calmly.

'Hmm, I don't really care if he understands or not,' Rose thought to herself. She was feeling just a little guilty about the way she was treating Travis. In the past she was such a sweet innocent person and had always treated everyone with the utmost consideration.

When Travis left he told Rose he'd be back in a couple of days, and begged her to give his proposal some consideration. She didn't want to seem rude, so she held her composure, smiling as she said goodbye to him. After he left Rose she called Garvin, and he explained that he met Travis at a stage show a few years back. Even so, it was up to her what decision she made. She did feel better knowing that he actually knew him. Rose got a phone call the day after Travis left. It was from a woman who introduced herself as Sandy, a singer who worked with Travis. She said that Travis had told her Rose was hard to convince but that he asked her to call because he was organizing a group together and they wanted Rose to come and join their team. She chatted on and on as if she would never stop. Rose listens patiently for a while, then half laughing over the phone, she said,

"Do you always talk so much.". Honestly, I think you could be an excellent sales woman."

"People are always saying that," Sandy answered. "Anyway, Travis is an honest man. I've known him for a few years now. We did a couple of shows together, but having a group would prove more beneficial. Besides having another female in the group would be good company for me and the team."

"Rose cut in, why me? Can't he find anyone else to fill this role?" Then reluctantly she added, "I don't think that I'm the right person you're looking for."

The conversation lasted for a while longer, and in the end Rose was half certain that Travis motives might be genuine.

"Meet us this weekend and see for yourself the things we do and then you can decide," Sandy urged.

"I`ll try my best," she told her; with that they said goodbye and the conversation ended.

Rose went to work the following day in a wonderful mood, and as soon as she stepped through the door she shouted,

"Pauline, come and let me fill you in, girl". Pauline was sitting around the back of the restaurant as usual in her favourite old, reliable chair.

"Rose I'm out here ,"she shouted back to her, "come on around here." Pauline was delighted, to see her friend looking so blissfully happy, as if she had won a million dollars, her smile stretching from ear to ear. She reached out to Rose and said,

"Come sit beside me. What got you looking like a shiny new penny?"

"A what?" Rose said, as she burst out laughing. Still giggling she said, "Your choice for words is rather peculiar these days, as if you're possessed by an old soul.

"Maybe I am," Pauline uttered,.

"Well I wouldn't doubt it, but let me explain what just happened." Rose went on to tell her about the phone call she'd had with Sandy.

She was cautious, didn't want to get her hopes up and then be left disheartened. After she'd told Pauline everything, her friend said that she believed it was for real, and urged her to go that weekend and see how it went. Rose placed her hand upon her head, and sighed.

"Alright, I'll give it chance, but this will be my last attempt", Rose warned as she walked off towards the restroom. The weekend came and Rose decided to travel to 'Ohio Rio', to see the group. When she got there, a woman was waiting for her at the bus station. She already knew what to expect, based on the conversation they had before.

"Hello Rose," she greeted her. "Nice to finally meet you."

Smiling shyly Rose said, "Hi Sandy". They then walk off together, with Sandy taking the lead, as Rose kept walking beside her. Sandy was a talker, asking a lot of questions. Rose noticed her attitude had changed; she wasn't planning on sticking around, she was searching for something better. They stopped, and Rose focussed on her.,

"Hold on! What's going on?"

"I have my daughter to care for. There isn't sufficient money in it anymore," Sandy responded, biting her nails.

"Why are you telling me this? Now I'm feeling betrayed.

"Please don't say anything to him," Sandy begged.

"Don't worry, I won't," Rose said, crossly. "I swear you people are jokers. Why did you call me if that was how you felt? Telling me how great everything was. Now this!"

"It was, but I'm not sure what's going on, myself. Travis isn't telling us anything," Sandy was now back-peddling, trying to protect her innocence.

"I`m already here. Might as well stay and see the outcome of this fiasco," Rose said as they' walked to a music studio where they met up with Travis. He was there waiting.

"Greetings Rose," he said as he shook her hand.

"hmm," she mumbled, making Travis look uneasy.

"Is everything alright? How was your journey?" He kept chatting.

" I`m doing good," Rose said, ignoring his gaze. Sandy caught Rose's eye when Travis wasn't looking and she whispered

"Please calm down,". Rose could see she the fear in her eyes, and felt a sudden hostility towards her, but then took pity and began reassuring the woman that she wouldn't repeat what she had told her. Travis was showing Rose the town, taking her into hotels that they`d performed in, and she believed he was trying very hard to impress her. Rose had never seen such a place before, so extravagant; there were tourists everywhere, strolling around in their swimwear. The ballrooms were filled with the most beautifully decorated tables. Travis was enquiring about gigs for the group, but Rose tried to compose herself; she wasn't one to show excitement. While Travis was meeting with the coordinator about performing at the hotel, Rose and Sandy kept talking between themselves about their future. Sandy, was hinting to Rose that maybe she was going to leave the group. Rose wasn't planning on staying long either but this was disappointing for her to hear, having not even started yet. However, Rose kept it to herself without revealing her intentions.. She saw it like a revolving door, repeating the same cycle. Rose assumed Travis wanted to replace Sandy, or did he genuinely need a second female, in his group she wondered?

The weekend came for the big event, Rose was to perform for the first time with the group. Rose went down to Ochi Rios early Saturday morning to rehearse with the band, and everyone was there, including

131

Sandy. It went well; they had four hours remaining before the show would begin so Travis took them all back to his house to freshen up and relax. His home was nice and modern; he lived there with his family, his wife and his daughter.

The stage show went well, better than expected but the payment didn't make it worth it, considering that Rose had to travel all the way from Kingston. It was a good experience but how far was she willing to go to pursue this dream of hers. Rose performed with the group for a few months, only on weekends. In the end Rose decided that she wasn't going to sacrifice everything for something that wouldn't be any benefit to her in long term; she had enough of all the nonsense. As much as Rose loved singing it was time to move on. Rose told Travis that she was leaving the group, and by then Sandy had already gone, but she kept in touch with Rose from time to time. Travis was displeased, but Rose wasn't asking his permission; it was a direct statement – she was leaving the group. His attempts in persuading Rose to stay fell on deaf ears; her mind was made up, there was no turning back. Travis wanted to stay in touch with Rose, although she wasn't too keen about the idea. This time Rose was ready, her old experience had given her the courage to move; she was disappointed but not devastated. During this time Rose was still working at Ms Peg's restaurant. It was now eight years she'd been with them. She knew that one day she would be leaving Ms Peg, and that one day was now imminent. She thought about the future and her prospects. She didn't want to let herself down again, she couldn't handle such adversity. It was sad enough watching the women in her community living such inadequate lives.

Rose was still living at Diane`s, and they had a really good connection between them. Everyone was supportive, and Rose loved and admired them equally. Even though it was Charmaine who had introduced her to the rest of the family Rose had grown fonder of Diane. She wouldn't change Charmaine for the world but that was just the way it was. They were all beautiful individuals and Rose wouldn't have asked for a more genuine family, but no one person is ever the same as another.

Rose realised she adored doing people's hair, making them feel beautiful.

"Pauline! I`m going to be a hairdresser." This time she seemed really confident with her decision. Pauline was always supportive when it came to Rose and her ambitions, especially knowing how hard she had worked since the day she had met her. Rose needed to find something positive to do, apart from working in the restaurant that was weighing heavily on her mind. Eventually Rose found a Hairdressing salon, where the lady who owned the business also taught the skills. Rose decided to attend, and she paid the fee for the course that lasted for six-months., Rose was a top student. She finally was going somewhere with her life. The woman offered her a part time job, working at the weekends. Rose did so well for herself. She was likeable, and so she was given the chance of working in a few other hair salons. After Rose finished her course she was presented with a certificate for her achievement. That was her second certificate she'd ever earned, the other one being the one she got from secondary school. Rose felt proud of her accomplishment. After a while she was able to work at home, and at the weekends. Her greatest delight was creating hairstyles and seeing the smiles on the customers' faces when she'd finished. Rose was still working with Ms Peg during the weekdays, and so she managed to save a few hundred dollars whenever she could. Diane's little business wasn't doing so great; her profit was next to nothing, but Rose was able to contribute more money towards the shopping.

Finally Rose decided it was time to visit her parents; Jenna was now living at Maria`s house, history repeating itself, except she hadn't run away from home. Living in the country everything seemed limited. After Jenna finished high school there wasn't much for her to do. Her desire was to be a nurse, but Rose's parents couldn't afford to send her to college, which was very sad. When Rose got to her family home everything was different about her situation. She wasn't a teenager any she'd learned many survival skills and had acquired more experience about the world outside than anyone else in her family. Rose spoke with her father, but nothing out of the ordinary; the fact was that she was staying at his house for few days, and didn't want to show any disrespect. It didn't feel the like home she remembered; she was like a stranger in a place that was once her home, and was now filled with nothing but sorrowful memories. Del was still living at home, and so was Verna who now had three other children residing there with her. Unfortunately, her children's father, had got sick and died tragically. It was a challenging time for her and that's when she went back home. Rose had known him years before, he was a good soul and she had got on fairly well with him. By then Willy had married his long-time girlfriend Carla, and they had built their home on the family land. In that way, he was closer to home. Willy had been facing a similar situation to Rose many years before, except now he wasn't living in the house anymore. Rose was delighted to see how far her brother had come, striving to make his way in the world.

He challenged Rose to a singing competition. He`d enjoyed a decent run himself, but wasn't any good at it, or so he thought.

"Rose," he said, his eyes opened wide, as if he'd just won the marathon, "I did well, didn't I, Sis". Rose burst into a fit of the giggles

"Yes bro', you the champion of the dancehall," she said sarcastically. He'd know that she was lying; it was a private joke that they shared. Every opportunity Willy got with Rose, was mostly about singing. In another life he would probably be a legend, she thought, as she smiled at him. At one point, he thought that he could become a famous rapper; maybe in another world, but in this one he was too shy. He was happy for Rose, though, and respected how hard she had endeavoured to overcome her tribulations and come through everything. Not once had Rose contemplated becoming a victim; she had always considered herself to be a survivor, strong and ready to live. Rose younger sisters and her brother Willy were always comfortable around each other; they were truthful, no cover ups, nor pretence. Del was delighted to see Rose, as they hadn't seen each other in a quite a while, their sisterhood connection was still there.

Rose wasn't afraid or scared anymore of her father; instead she stayed focused like a solider preparing for the battlefield. While Rose was away her father's behaviour had sometimes been outrageous. From time to time Del would call Rose in Kingston, informing her of some of the awful things that he did. She would be so angry at him, knowing that after all those years the old man was still creating havoc. When she arrived on her visit Rose brought something for everyone, small gifts that everyone was pleased to receive, especially as they came from Kingston. A few times during Rose's stay her dad got hammered, but nothing compared to years before when she was still living there. Soon it was time for Rose to returned to Kingston, back to a life that she had grown all too ever familiar with.

The morning before she was ready to leave, her dad went into his yam field and he came back with a basketful of yams on his head for her to take home with her. He didn't say much, but she knew deep down he cared. Buying food was expensive in Kingston, most people couldn't afford to purchase even a piece of yam so she appreciated his gift. She said her goodbye,; making a point of thanking her dad. This visit had been much better that the previous and , everyone was sad to see her go, but she had her own life now and she had to return to it. A few hours later Rose was on the road travelling back to Kingston. She felt unburdened, knowing that she was her own person, could move around without any restrictions, and more importantly there wasn't any new dilemmas facing her.

A few years later, Ricky's mother died. She fell ill and her feeble body was incapable of enduring it; she also suffered a fall that forced her into a state of incontinence. Poor woman! Anyone could see how exhausted she had become but after a couple of years, battling the odds, she passed away. It was devastating when she died, especially for Ricky and his daughter; she was their main confidant and the backbone of their family. Jenna was staying there for a while, but eventually went back home. While she'd stayed with Maria she mostly worked in the shop, and business was blooming like never before. She was beautiful, like a morning Lilly that remains fresh even when there`s no rain to keep it alive. There were men coming from near and far to purchase goods from the shop, just to gaze on her beauty, but she wasn't interested in them. After a year or less Jenna went back to their parents' home. Maria begged her to return, as she'd been the primary source of their business been successful. She went back and it wasn't long after that Del came to stay there too. Unfortunately, after attending school for years there wasn't any exciting opportunity waiting for them; their destiny was totally up to them. Del happened to be passionate about clothing design, and was given the chance of completing her studies at a sewing and textile school. Rose knew that they had all been affected by their past life, of witnessing the things that they had, for years. Del went on to be amazing at what she did, making and designing beautiful clothing for women and was always hoping that she would have her own beauty boutique. Rose was hoping that with the talent that she had she'd get a fair chance and eventually she did. did well by herself. She worked hard to accomplish being the best, but sadly nothing in life is free. The people who try the hardest sometimes in life, don't often got the support they need.

CHAPTER 8
A NEW WORLD OF MOTHERHOOD

Like so many women before her, Rose became a single unmarried mother. At the time, it was common for a young woman to have children without' jumping over the broom'. Rose met the man of her dreams, or so she thought, but then later that transformed her life forever, but not in the way she had imagined. Calvin was his name; a good looker, he worked as an engineer fixing trailer trucks over at the boat factory, next door to Ms Pegs restaurant. He would usually come over at lunchtime to purchase his meal. He was tall, dark, and handsome, just as she always imagined the man of her dreams to be, except this was no fairy tale. He had the most charming smile. They became friends, sharing jokes, and doing things together; she was impressed with his manners, but above all things, she hadn't met anyone like him before. He was transfixed by her beauty and personality, and eventually they started dating. He was at the restaurant, basically, every evening before she went home. Rose felt fortunate to have someone who admired her in such an adoring way. As the months went on Rose was in heavenly bliss, and believed that perhaps she had found her prince, minus the white horse, and she was ready to share him with a few of her family members.

Jenna and Del were the first to be enlightened about the marvellous new man in Rose 's life, and they were pleased for her. Eventually, after months of getting to know him better and becoming sure that he was 'the one' she called Maria and told her about him And she, too, was pleased for Rose. Eventually the weekend came when she finally took him to visit her sister in the country. He was welcomed wholeheartedly and made an excellent impression, displaying his finest qualities. Rose was overjoyed! The weekend was a success. Monday morning, they were back off to Kingston.

Calvin always seemed to carry a sadness about with him. He sometimes seemed a little detached which he told Rose was due tohis dilemma regarding his mother's absence in his life as a child. He told Rose that he was brought up by his dad and that he hadn't met his mother until he was 20 years old. It was obvious how it had affected him. Rose would often listen to specific comments he would make during their conversations, Which seemed to have nothing to do with what she had been talking about. He talked a lot about his siblings and their upbringing. Rose heard the disappointment in his voice that he had towards his mother. Rose encouraged him to still love his mother, regardless. Later she understood it wasn't all his mother's fault. His dad was part of the predicament, driving her away, but that didn't seem to make any change regarding the situation, or to Calvin's dejected mood when he spoke about her.

About almost a year into their relationship, Rose fell pregnant. She was scared, but felt confident that Calvin wouldn't abandon her and their baby, considering it was the first child for them both. He was excited at first, then he went into what she thought of as standby mode. Suddenly the cracks started to appear, the signs were too clear to avoid. Rose tried to convince herself that he was trying to do the fatherly thing, as he was expected to do. At this time, Rose was still working for Ms Peg, but she had morning sicknesses, and some days she was unable to go into work, and had to stay home. Calvin said he came around as much as he could, but used work as an excuse to not always be there, thinking that she wasn't aware of what was happening. Rose would often ask him if everything was alright, and he kept saying yes, but still his actions were confirming his behaviour. She worked and saved her money, until she was eight months pregnant, when her sixth sense was telling her that she should be ready; she had witnessed her older sisters being let-down in the same way and knew the signs. She wasn't sure how she would cope, but one thing her struggles had taught her was resilience. During her seventh month he hadn't been around either financially or emotionally, but lucky for her she had a back-up plan if the first didn't work out. She was worried; deep down in her stomach she could feel that he was going to desert her, that she was going to become a single mom. Rose had to learn how to develop a mental support strategy, one that would keep her from going insane.

Rose focussed all her energy on the baby and herself, and in fact Pauline, Diane and the others were there for her as well. It was customary to buy clothing for the unborn baby during the seventh month, of pregnancy she was inclined to do the same but there were complications on Calvin's part. He didn't seem to comprehend the fact that he must live up to his responsibilities, and consequently there was no contribution from him either emotionally or financially. Rose felt so utterly alone, and would usually cry whenever no one was watching, blaming herself for being so stupid, allowing herself to believe in someone who wasn't worth it. "How didn't I see that coming," she asked. Diane felt nothing but pity towards him. "Cuz, don't blame yourself. These things happen. They shouldn't, but life is uncertain, and so are some men"."

"Everyone believes we`re the perfect couple. What do I say when they start asking question?" she asked.

"Listen," Diane interrupt her, "it's none of their business, and beside who give them the right to criticize you?"

"We're here for you, just don't stress yourself."

Rose couldn't respond because she knew Diane was saying the right things, and she felt fortunate to have her friendship. Rose told Diane and the others that she was going to meet Calvin, in Half-Way-Tree, for money to purchase baby clothing. Charmaine kept asking and she didn't know what to say. Even though Rose had met Charmaine first, Rose became much closer to Diane, but she did care for them equally.

"Do you want me to come with you," Diane asked protectively. Rose was glad that she had offered but still she refused.

"No, I`ll be alright thanks". In truth, Rose wasn't going to meet anyone, but in fact, sadly, she went to the bank instead to withdraw her own cash. Rose accepted her fate, sure that she was doing the right thing by herself. It was too shameful to even contemplate people's reactions, if they knew the truth. Rose was hoping that in time, he would do the right thing and give her some cash, and then she would be able to transfer it back it into her account. Sadly, that didn't happen; it was like looking for rain in a desert. When she got back Diane and the others were excited, but Rose returned with a heavy heart, full of her own deceptiveness. She showed them the money that she had withdrawn, and told them Calvin, had given it to her. From that moment, Rose acknowledged that he was now just a memory of her past. Mentally she had to be ready, but was that enough to keep her motivated to carry on? Rose found the from somewhere . Calvin came to visit a few more times before she had the baby, but it was like something had turned the lights off from his soul. He was always feeling sorry for himself, justifying reasons for his financial problem but Rose stopped listening. He was damaged, and she couldn't give him the comfort he wanted. Rose needed everything she had for herself and her baby; her resentment was building up towards him.

The baby within Rose was fully developed, and she was ready to give birth. That day she got up and had a shower, but she wasn't feeling her usual self; a new beginning was dawning. She had attended all her clinic appointments and seen the doctor, so she knew she should be ok. Her suitcase with her everything she would need had been packed and ready, since she reached seven months. Her body was exhausted and tired, after supporting and nourishing her baby for nine months. She was now entering labour; Calvin was seemingly in hiding. Diane went and got a taxi to carry Rose to the hospital. She accompanied her there, and waited with her, until it was time for Rose to see the doctor. It was difficult for her, not knowing what to expect. Diane was unable to stay at the hospital but came back the following day. The experience was nothing like Rose had anticipated.

the nurses were calling mothers on the ward to be examined by the doctors. When it came around to Rose's turn, she hesitated, her heart pumping into full speed. Mothers' cries were melodramatic while giving birth, their voices and screams were unbearable to listen to. Rose began praying to herself, 'please God, don't let me die today.' The nurse called her name twice.

"I`m here," she said uncertainly.

"Come with me miss, the nurse smiled kindly. Rose walked slowly towards her, beginning to hyperventilate, but the nurse reassured her with "it's going to be fine," as she gently touched her shoulders. She went into the doctor's room. 'Oh my god' she thought, he must have the largest hands, and fingers, I've ever seen'. The examination was just as awful as she'd expected it to be. Rose was in excruciating pain, and she was sent to a bed inside a bay. It wasn't fancy, and from her vantage point she could see some of the mothers giving birth; nothing was sacred anymore, nothing was off limits.

Rose believed that she was dying.

"Please don't let me die," she kept repeating over and over aloud, as a lovely nurse held her hand and reassured Rose that she would live through this.

"You can squeeze my hands whenever the pain gets too intense," the nurse told her. The ward was filled with the noises of women giving birth, some of whom were using profound language making it confusing to think. After the ordeal was over, Rose was handed the most beautiful baby boy on the planet. She loved him instantly, so tiny and delicate, she thought as he looked at him closely for the first time. He was perfect in every way; the following morning Diane came back to visit Rose and her son, and was excited to know that they both were doing well. That same evening Rose went home. She named her son, Neil. Diane would walk him early in the morning, while Rose was sleeping.

Calvin came the following week to visit them, and she could tell by his face that he was half frightened to death, but Rose had no intention of withholding from him the right to see his son. He had been a poor excuse of a father, while his son was in the womb but that wouldn't make any difference now, Rose thought as she glanced at him. He picked Neil up, smiling like a clown, and finally said,

"Sorry I couldn't be here any sooner, at which Rose nodded with a frown. He brought with him, a pack of nappies and a few hundred dollars, and for the first time, watching him, she knew he wasn't going to be around for them for long. However, she acted with such conviction, Rose wanted him to see that she was strong, brave and a good mother.

"Next week I`m going to register Neil's birth. Will you accompany me to the registry officer"? Rose asked Calvin, with such a tone in her voice that he couldn't say anything. "Yes," he responded. She wanted him to feel some type of remorse.

Rose didn't want to wait too long before she registered Neil's birth, so she took the earliest appointment that the office had available, which was on Monday of the following week. She told him where to meet her, Rose kept on open mind, in case he disappointed her but to her surprise he was waiting for them when she got there. The day went well, much better than she had anticipated, but she hadn't forgotten how he treated her, insisting he had taken every precaution as far as he was concerned. The birth certificate would be ready to collect in a few weeks after the procedure was done. Calvin was to accompany Rose and the baby back to her house, spending, as he claimed, the rest of the day bonding. She thought maybe he was trying to be a good dad but deep-down Rose was unable to shake that feeling off. 'Hmm, dearest lord have mercy upon me. I can see the road won`t be easy, but I`m depending on you, amen,' she whispered to herself as she sat there watching him with Neil. He left later, saying that he would bring some stuff by the following week.

"OK," she answered, rubbing her feet together. Rose wasn't expecting anything different, so when he didn't turn up, she wasn't surprised. Not till a month later did he appear again, his mouth filled with more ridiculous excuses.

"You work all day but never seem to get paid. Who does that?" Rose demanded to know.

He held his head down, looking at the ground, as if he is awaiting money to pop up out to him.

"I can`t keep doing this with you. Ever since I got pregnant you`ve been a dead loss". Rose was upset to the edge of tears. She breathed deeply closing her eyes, then exhaled, counting down her heart beats slowly. Rose then cleared her throat.

"For God's sake, can you not say something?"

Calvin stood there with an intense stare in on his face, then responded,

"I am trying. The people that I`m working with will pay me money soon." Rose sat down on an old chair at the side of Diane's house.

"So, you think this is all about money? Honesty, I feel sorry for you. You come around whenever it pleases you, Neil, will never know who you are".

Neil was inside sleeping; he walked towards the door looked inside at him, and whispered,

"he's sleeping so I won't wake him." Calvin looked directly at Rose, who told him,

"Yes, just go now.".

"OK then. `I`ll be by at the weekend."

She didn't answer but went and laid beside her baby son. She could hear Calvin as he walked off, but Rose felt like such a fool at this point that it didn't matter anymore.

Diane's other sister lived in a big yard, and the owner of the land lived in a three bedroom old wooden house. The owner had known Rose when she worked at Ms Peg's restaurant. Everyone called him Mr Gus, and although he never did have a wife or children he just got on with life. Over the years that Rose worked at Ms Peg restaurant he was there every single day to collect his dinner. It was clear that he wasn't one to cook. It was always the same thing – fried chicken, and rice and peas; Rose used to believe he might start growing feathers one day. He was polite and had good manners, like an old soul from a different time. He had an extra room that wasn't occupied, and he offered it to her on a monthly rent. It was cheap enough so Rose took it. By this time Rose didn't go back to work, she just wanted to take care of her son. While she was off on maternity leave, Ms Peg paid her for four months; she couldn't afford six months payment, she told Rose apologetically. Rose knew at some point, it would happen.

Now with a son to maintain, and a father who didn't know what time of day it was, she was on her own. Of course Diane and the family did the best they could. Rose already was preparing herself for this day, ever since been pregnant. Her son was now six months old, and moving around like a little ninja; he really was the cutest little baby, and always cheerful. Rose loved him from the moment he was born, calling him her Poo Bear. Most of the time Diane, or Charmaine would be with him, giving Rose time to focus on her plans. The day came when Rose was organising her new home, it was slightly bigger than Diane's place, but wasn't anything extravagant. She brought a tin of paint to freshen up the old place. She did it all herself; she didn't ask for assistance from anyone. It was tiring, and when Diane's brother came by he asked,

"Cuz, why didn't you request my help?" as he took the paint bush out of Rose's hand. "I'd a notion that probably you were busy," she smiled. Another man came by carrying a paint brush, too, "Rose, I heard that you needed help with your painting," he said. "Yeah, you're doing a nice job here," he said as he strolled into the wooden room, wielding the painting brush like he was a real artist. In no time they'd completed it and Rose was grateful to both of them.

"Let the smell of the paint evaporate before you settle in" they advised.

146

"Alright, thanks for telling me," Rose answered, although in reality she already knew that. Her parents always painted their house at Christmas, so she wasn't a stranger to such activity.

The day went according to plan. Rose than placed a bucket of water in the middle of the room to evaporate the odour. She needed a few bits furniture to add, to fill the empty space. She already had a bed frame but needed a mattress. She eventually moved in two days later after Rose and Diane went in to Kingston to purchase the other thing that she required. It was traditional to use frankincense, sea salt and other essences, which should be burnt in a bowl, before moving in and so that is what she did. Rose and Neil finally moved in, and Diane seemed saddened, but Rose was delighted to have her own place; independence at last.

Everyone was now living in the circle; Rose could throw a stone on the top of Diane's house. The front of the house had a lot of loose dirt, that appeared to be desert sand and her front door was exposed to its dreadful fury. During the days she would sprinkle the surface with water, and most of time prayed that it would rain.

Mr Gus was an odd character; he stayed in his own corner. He had a strange way, of doing things, in particular , brushing his teeth was one of them.

Every morning at the same time, a blast of sound would come from his moth like an old goat hanging from a hillside. He would push his toothbrush so far back into this throat that you'd think he would be guaranteed to suffer a horrible death in time. Some of the children called him Santa Claus, because of his full facial hair, long and white like snow. Rose had her suspicions about him; he liked younger girls, and although he tried to keep it a secret, people were talking. To Rose he was a dirty old man, but in spite of that discomfort, Rose felt at peace. It was now months that Calvin hadn't visited Rose and their son; it was hard, but she was adjusting to the situation. She was no longer living at Diane`s, but he didn't even know that she and the baby had moved .Calvin was now a stranger, who used to turn up whenever he pleased, mouthing the same old excuses all the time, until eventually Rose had had enough of his pathetic behaviour: that was when she lived at Diane's place. Rose knew that at some point, he would appear again, no matter how long it took him. This time she was ready for him; she went into one of her deep meditations where she analysed her life, thoroughly. 'This isn't working out for us; you're under no circumstances involved in our lives; each time you come around your mind seems to be somewhere else; its best we go our separate ways; doesn't make any difference because you haven't been here; you got no devotion as a father'. All these thoughts passed through her head until she decided, 'yes, I'll say that to him if ever he returns. It was like practicing a script, revising it constantly until it become your truth. He had friends that knew them together, and they spoke to him about his fatherly responsibilities, but instead of rectifying his ways, he became rebellious and terminated their friendship.

Calvin hadn't been around for months, and at one-point Rose thought that something horrible might have happened to him. She wasn't entirely heartless towards him, even under the troubles she and her son endured. He had his own issues, and it wasn't her job to fix him; he was trapped in his own world, fighting whichever demons he had got there. They say life has many unexpected trials and tribulations waiting for when one least expects them and so it was for the people of their community. Another gang war surfaced, this time even more abominable than anything Rose had experienced before. People were

148

killed from both side, and friends turned against each other. The community that Rose, resided in wasn't involved, but they were again stuck in the middle; used as a hiding ground at nights for wicked men. Everyone kept indoors, but didn't feel much safer as the walls were built from plyboard – you could be indoors and still be shot. The surrounding area was like a garden, all the flowers were familiar with each other in some way, and yet different to a certain degree.

One particular night it had been raining earlier in the evening, and that carried on throughout the night. The zinc rooves were standing their ground, but as the rain beat against the old wooden frames, every sound of movement was easily detected from nearby. First it was a battle between the wind and the rain, but suddenly there were voices. Rose held her breath, anticipating what was going to emerge next. One of the voices was all too familiar, and Rose had an insight that things were about to get dangerous.

"Who lives here," one said.

"It's Rose that works at the restaurant down on the high road," the other responded.

"Call her, so she can let us in. This rain is getting worse," an unfamiliar voice insisted.

"No, I won't do that, the woman is sleeping," protest the recognisable voice.

Rose's heart was beating like a magical drum out of control. 'Jesus!' was the only thought that went through her mind, as she trembled in fear, thinking the worst. She nervously climbed off the bed, and you could have heard the bones in her body creaking, she was being so quiet. Lifting her baby from the bed and kneeling on the hard, wooden floorboards, Rose pulled the blankets off the bed, and placed them on the floor under the bed. She then lay there with baby Neil close beside her, like a mother bird safeguarding her young. The baby was still slumbering, and Rose was glad as his crying would have alerted them that she was awake; luckily he had always slept well during the night. As she lay frozen to the floor, Rose talked with god,

"I know I`m unable to see you, but I believe you're always here with me' Surely there must be a better way for us; what life can I possible give to my son, living in such a place as this. I`ve been suffering these tribulations all my life, and sometimes I felt like giving up, but what good would come to me if I did?"

She stared into the darkness, watching and waiting for her front door to be kicked in at any moment, clutching her son to her breast. In the silence, in all the madness Rose was sure she heard voices inside the room, but it was just figments of her imagination. Eventually the rain stopped beating on the old, resilient roof top, and a ray of light appeared through the cracks in the house. She felt tired and drained, having not slept at all during that long, long night.

There was a knocking on Rose's front door, and at first she pretended not to hear it, she wasn't sure if it was worth answering.

"Rose," the person called out her name, and she dragged herself from the floor as she realised it was Diane and her friend, Nada, who lived across the road. She opened the door, seemingly restless.

"Are you and the baby OK?" Everyone was speaking all at once, having had similar encounters; Rose didn't see the need to answer, just waited patiently for her turn. They shoved their way into the room where Neil was still sleeping on the floor wrapped up all cosy like a teddy bear; he had no concept of the night's horror. Rose dropped her head down onto her knees.

"Cuz you alright?"

"Hmm. Not really, haven't had a nap all night, and my head is aching badly." Neil woke up as Nada, picked him up off the floor. She held him in her arms, and he kept smiling at her.

"Oh, if he only knew! Such innocence. I need to protect him," Rose said slowly gazing at her son. They'd had a disastrous night, obviously there were still more scumbags hiding outside, petrifying people in their homes; even the men in the community were reserved and not talking. Diane offered Rose a cup of lemon tea.#

"Thank you," she said. She placed it on the tiny glass table that stood in the corner a of the room. It was now about nine o clock in the morning, and Neil needed his bath – he had one every day at the same time and this was no different. After Nada bathed Neil, Rose made him a bottle.

"Please can you hold him, while I go have a shower. My brain is on fire and I have to calm my body down."

"Yeah, no problem, I`ll carry him, to my house. Come over when you've finished," Nada said, walking off with the baby.

The bathroom was a tiny shack; Rose had thought it was horrendous at first, but after living there for a while she programmed her mind to take possession of her surroundings. The one good thing about it was its open space giving a vision of everything that moved. No one was able to see her while she had a shower, despite it having no roofing. However, Rose was able see whoever passed by through the cracks and holes of its shabby frame. She had a shower and went back to her room. The outside seemed grubby and old, but inside was home for Rose and her son. She quickly dressed and went by to Nada's house. Neil was crawling around on the floor, as happy as a sunflower. She stood there just looking at him and Nada signalled her to come inside. They talked until Rose was tired and ready to leave.

151

"I'm going away for a while," she said as she bent to pick up her son.

"where are you going," Nada said, sounding surprised.

"Country, to see my family. It's been a long time coming. Neil is now six months old and I believe I should go."

" I think you're right. You need a take a break from all this madness," Nada said, throwing her hands into the air like a rag doll, shaking her head in agreement.

"I'm leaving this weekend," and Rose told her, smiling.

"O,K" Nada responded as they walked back to Rose's house. She was suddenly feeling ravenous,

"Going to cook some food before I lie down."

"Oh, that's a good idea, I'll come and help you." Rose was pleased, as she said to Nada,

"Come on then, let's go." Nada took the baby from Rose arms, still chatting away. She always had a lot to say, and only lived a minute away. It wasn't long before they'd completed their master chef dish. Nada was a good cook, always trying out new things; she dreamt of having her own restaurant some day in the future. Rose, herself, cooked well, especially after her years of experience working at Ms Peg's, but never had any desire to have that as a profession.

Rose told Diane and the others that she was going to visit her family. Diane wasn't surprised.

"So Cuz, how long are you staying away"? she said as she picked at some peas she had in a pot.

"Hmm, a few weeks I think, depending on how it goes. "I haven't seen them for a while now and my father and I aren't on good terms, but still, I'll take my chances. In fact, whatever will be, will be.".

" Nothing will happen," Diane's sister remarked.

" Yeah, I know. Leaving this weekend."

"O", Diane said, as she took the baby from Rose. "Two days from now, I'm going to miss you guys, particularly the baby." Rose just smiled, then sat down on a chair outside the front door of Diane's place. The weekend came quickly, and Rose, was ready as much as she could be. She became stronger and more courageous; life's lesson had taught her endurance was an important part of life. She went downtown to catch the bus for her journey. It was sticky, humid, and dry and everything appeared like she was in the desert, with piles of rubbish in every corner. Vendors lining the streets on both sides, creating obstructions for those walking by. Finally Rose and her baby were on a bus. She sat at the window seat near the back; Neil was behaving well and never seemed to bother about much, except when he was hungry or needed his wet nappies changing. 'Wow! Rose thought', how impressive! So many big houses being built all around, people are improving on their status.

Soon Rose's lengthy journey ended and she held her baby in her arms, placing his head across her shoulder, as she alighted from the bus. The conductor kindly helped her to the other side of the street with her baggage. Rose looked around curiously; she hadn't been here in years and it all looked very different from before. Now they had taxis.

"Are you ready miss," – Rose didn't recognise the driver or see anyone that she recognised. Most had relocated to different places and then came back and upgraded their community; it was splendid to see. The taxi took Rose home. The driver knew her mother apparently, as they were related. She could see that he was young, and he must have been just a juvenile when she left home ages ago. Surprisingly, no one was sitting on the veranda as they always had, the grocery shop door wasn't opened, but the side window was. The dogs came around barking in a friendly fashion. Del and Jenna weren't residing at home any more, as they were staying at Maria's. Every two weeks Rose's dad would make sure to send bags of his produce from his cultivation for them; he did the best he could. Verna, had moved back home with her children because their dad had died. Rose knocked on the front door of the house, she had once called home; it was looking the same, except it had been freshly painted. Her mother came to the door,

" Oh my god! Rose!" she cried. She was practically in tears. They had heard she had a baby, but this was the first time they'd seen her since then. Everyone was thrilled at seeing Rose, even her dad, when he came home.

"Hey, Rose, you finally came to spend time with us, so I can get to know my grandson," he said appearing pleased as punch.

Everyone was connected, as if she hadn't ever left. They'd already eaten dinner but Rose's mom always had crackers and bread in the house.

"Let me get you a cup of mint tea, and some water crackers with some cheese."

Neil was a well behaved baby, and so adorable. Verna made him a bottle, and he drank it hungrily. Rose was settling in smoothly, and they talked for hours, laughing and having a good time. She went by Willy's house, which wasn't far from her parents' house as it was built on the family land. Rose and Willy's wife were close friends, they shared jokes about the good, and bad, old days. The first week went well; her dad seemed to be in control of himself, and hadn't had a drink, or maybe he did – who knows? – but nothing out of the ordinary. Rose was pleased with his behaviour, and was anticipating that her father would remain as sober as a judge for the rest of time she and the baby were visiting. Her second week started out well, but Oh! how trouble sneaks up when you least expect it. He was still living over his domain; his choice. It was reaping time in the fields as usual, and after a week of hard labour, toiling away on the land, it was the honourable custom that people engaged in, to let their hair down at the end of it. Even he wasn't exempt from having a good time, but for him the enjoyment was short lived; the drink drove him into madness. Rose's mind was troubled; all his drinking entourage were having a grand time at his expense, as well as taking his stock without payment. When their appetite was satisfied some would slowly slip away like snakes on a cold rainy day, and when there were no one left to entertain, his attention was directed at his family but not in a pleasant way. It was late at night, and you'd think he might go to his bed, but if that's what you thought you'd be mistaken

That night, the shouting and yelling were evidence of his self-indulgence.

Rose and the baby had been sleeping in her mother's, bedroom with her since she the beginning of the visit.

"Oh God, I hope he doesn't come over here, not while he`s in that way," she said to her mother feeling restless. Despite the darkness she could see the discontent on her mother's face. Suddenly he was banging on the front window, and yelling unpleasant words that triggered Rose's memories.

"How can he still have all this energy after all these years," Rose sighed.

"Move away from the window before you break it," Rose's mom called out to him.

Well, some people would go sleep on it, but not him, being the sort of person that he was. He wasn't pleased with her remark and decided he needed to enter the house by any means possible; bang, banging, you would think there was an army trying to get in. No one was jumping ropes to let him in, certainly not Rose, and her mother was getting nervous about his behaviour escalating. His persistent disturbance became worse, and in the end Rose's mother eventually went and opened the door for him. He shoved past her like a cyclone, ready to create havoc. She quickly came back into the bedroom, hopped in the bed, while he then made himself at home sitting in the dining room cursing. But he wasn't satisfied about the result, so, he proceeded towards the bedroom.

Standing near the doorway of her mothers' room, he kicked on the door until it flew open slamming back hard against the wall. At this Rose was furious at him but kept silent, but her mother however, was asking him to leave; the noise was frightening the baby and the other children in the house. Her plea was falling on deaf ears, and he proceeded to toss her stuff across the room, with no regard for anything or anyone. It was now do or die; Rose had had enough, her silence became rage; she had never felt such anger towards anyone in her entire life. To her he wasn't her father but an intruder trying to finish off what he had started, and Rose wasn't going to allow that to happen. She didn't want to physically, harm him and that wasn't her intention. In that moment, he saw her in a different light, Rose wasn't afraid of her father anymore; she had an episode where her spirit ascended from her body, throbbing like thunder in a storm. He turned and ran, as she chased him around the dinner table and then he was out the door like a rocket.

CHAPTER 9
DECISION TIME, NO RETURN

The following day, it become apparent that he was still angry, especially at Rose. The funny thing was that he was able to remember how afraid she made him feel. He stood in the doorway that led to his grocery shop, but wouldn't come any closer and one would assume that he was still hammered because of the awful things that he was saying. His demeaning words cut sharper than a knife slicing through her very heart, like a bullet from a gun. The tears kept flowing down her face, as she looked at him from across the yard thinking he must be losing his mind. How can a parent be so malicious and hateful?

"What have I ever done to you old man?" she shouted at him.

It wasn't ideal, arguing with your parent; it felt wrong in every way, so Rose walked off away from his presence. At that moment, all she felt towards him was pity, and for the first time, Rose saw her mother supporting her. She didn't know where it came from, but her courage was clear to see. Rose concluded that the best thing to do would be to dismiss him from her mind, and then her heart – that would be her best solution.

She told herself her father would become a figment of her past; she buried him there but that wasn't so easy, she had to find a balance. Subsequently, there was silence as he went into his bedroom, and everyone thought that probably he was asleep. Rose was now in deep thought, directing her focus on what had happened; it was hard for her to comprehend it. "You won't see me for a long time. This will never happen again," she said to her mother with a stern face.

"Please don't say that Rose. How are we going to see you?

"Hmm" she sighed. I`ll figure something out but I can't think just now, mama". They spoke for a while, but Rose's mother couldn't convince her otherwise. No one saw him up until the following morning, and his awkwardness was a sign he was aware of what he had done, even though he didn't comment. The day went on as normal, while Rose reflected on her discission, that she had to make. There were whispers amongst them, as the rest of the family in the household were still in shock. Rose remained quiet for most of the day, her son was her main concern. The following day Rose decided to leave; it wasn't time, but she couldn't bear staying there another day, so she was ready to return back to Kingston. One thing she was happy about was that her mother wasn't a weak and frightened woman anymore.

They all talked, except for the person who was supposed to, but that was alright; she didn't want to have a conversation with him anyway. He went to his farm in the morning, and by the time he came back Rose and her baby were gone. The journey to Kingston was different; it opened up old wounds that she thought she had buried. Rose had a son to care for and nothing would prevent her from accomplishing that. She was trying to be the best mother that she could. The sun was clearer and brighter than ever before, and Rose felt a sense of relief knowing that she didn't have to prove anything anymore. Except reconciliation, but that wasn't possible now, although maybe one day – who knows?. It was now evening and she and the baby were back home Diane, and the rest of the family were delighted that they had returned.

Pauline had never visited Rose during her time of living with Diane, although she worked at the restaurant almost to the end of her pregnancy. Rose thought that maybe she would come after she had the baby. Sadly, Pauline blamed Diane for Rose leaving, and she didn't hide her feelings about her dislike towards her. It didn't make any sense to Rose, because Pauline knew the real reasons why she left but she was entitled to her feelings. However, she visited Rose probably twice after she left Diane's house. Rose didn't hold it against her, and they remained friends, but it wasn't like before. Rose had enough, to worry about herself, and that wasn't going to be one of them. Nada, too, was glad to see them; she quickly filled Rose in with all the local gossip that she had missed while she was away. However, there wasn't much to report; instead, Rose had a lot to tell them. Charmaine was choking with laughter during Rose's interpretation of the falling out with her dad; and by then, even Rose found it humorous.

The weeks became months, and Calvin still didn't come back. Rose presumed he had now burnt all his bridges with her. But then, unexpectedly he turned up. He had no clue that she and the baby had moved. Rose was washing some clothing, when Diane escorted him over to her current dwelling place; she hadn't expected to ever see him again. He seemed apprehensive, and she was rather agitated by his presence.

"Why are you here?" she asked without looking at him, as she continued with the washing. Rose remained in control of herself without showing any sign of aggression. Before he could reply she said, "Neil is inside sleeping; you can go see him if you wish". He obeyed and up the stairs he went. He had a bag in one hand but it didn't appear like it had much in it. She watched him as he climbed the stairs without realizing she was observing him. He seemed to be behaving like they were still together .'He must think I`m stupid!' Rose thought to herself, but she'd spent months of rehearsing what she would say to him and now was the perfect time to play it out.

He came out of the room with the baby in his hands, and Rose wasn't best pleased because when he`d gone she would have to deal with it.

"I could stay with him, until you're finished with the washing!".

"Oh," she replied thinking to herself that he'd no idea what awaited him. They didn't speak any more, his attention was mostly focusing on the baby. In her mind Rose figured his coming wasn't acceptable.

"So, are you doing alright?" he asked timidly, watching as she hung the clothing out on the line to dry!

"Yeah, doing fabulous," was her genuine answer to his question. She threw the wastewater across the yard, controlling the whirlwind of dust. He was on the move as soon as he saw that Rose had completed her task. She cleared her throat, and he looked down to the ground avoiding her stare. Rose's heart kept throbbing intensely, but her mind was made up, she couldn't turn back now. She hesitated for a brief second questioning herself, before she added, "don't come back, you're not even a part time dad". Her voice was undoubtedly steady as a rock. His expression showed his dismay but at the same time he's been expect it, he didn't even object.

"Are you sure this is what you want?" Now he had her full attention; she was trying to process his response and for a moment she almost fell for it. He looked so immensely trusting, but she'd been down this road before.

"Yes" she answers confidently; Rose was a show girl, she could pull off anything; she had a collection of masks and she wore different one each day.

Rose was now working from home, in her small wooden room that she shared with her son. Sometimes she would sit the customers on the narrow washed out porch, but closer on her side. Neil was at home with his mother at all times except on those occasions when Diane or Charmaine would come get him. He was a well behaved boy, and so they all adored him. Occasionally, Rose would withdraw a little back up from her savings. They visited each other every day, and that meant a lot to Rose.

The only mask, she couldn't wear well was the upset one; within a minute he was gone, through the zinc gates to the street that led to his freedom. Six months had passed by and no one had known whether or not he was in the land of the living. After a while Rose had accepted that he wasn't coming back, not for her or for his son. Rose loved and protected her son with everything thing she knew how. They were doing rather well and Rose was contented with the life she'd established together with her son. He was growing fast. She wanted more for them; her ambition opened windows allowing her to view the world differently. Rose dreamt that one day she and her son would leave the slums to a more uplifting area. Everything required money, and that too was diminishing out of her grasp. Rose was getting more hairstyling done, and the customers were pleased with her creativeness. The area wasn't flourishing with cash, the residents hardly had enough to buy food for their family, let alone, having a lavish hairdo on a weekly basis. Neil was now over a year old, filled with energy and always on the move, especially now that he was walking.

Neil had a real connection with Diane, and she loved him dearly. Unfortunately, she couldn't conceive children of her own. All her acquaintances and friends had children of their own, and she often said, "Oh, I have sufficient nieces and nephews," but you could see it was an act. There wasn't anything she could do, accepting her path was her way of moving forward. She once said, stressing over the things that she couldn't change would only cause more heartache; it was better that way.

Rose felt sorry for her, and so they never spoke about the topic, Rose didn't want to keep reminding her of such pain. Rose needed a job, but returning to Ms Peg's restaurant wasn't something she desired to do; it was like going backwards. So, she ventured out, pursuing vacancies that were available. Eventually Rose got a job in a hair salon but it wasn't very busy, the area was profoundly slow for business plus the payment was less than she was used to getting, even when working at the restaurant. Sonia frequently paid her in instalments, owing her the balance until the following week.

Sonia also had a grocery shop, and someone else came in for few day's work there. Sometimes it was only one customer, for the entire day. Sonia then suggested that Rose could start washing her clothes instead, to make up time. Rose wasn't happy working as her washer woman but she needed the money. Diane was able to help out with Neil, allowing Rose the opportunity to work; she got another job working at the local school in the area selling a mixture of things to the children. The good thing was that there was nearly always a family member home to look after Neil, but if not, Nada was more than glad to step in. Nada had her own children to care for, so Rose didn't want to burden her even though they're friends. . It was just for a day or two, Rose had to put her child first, her obligations were providing for him and herself. She worked hard to provide, her worse fear was being unable to obtain a job, and have to become a stay home mom doing nothing, like many of the other women in the area. Pauline came to visit her on a few occasions; they kept in touch and besides they were just living several metres away. Diane's sister, Charmaine, worked there for a year after Rose left, and then she, too, resigned from her job. Rose hated working at the hairdressers , so she was eager to find new employment but that proved more complicated than she thought. Her boss was a chatter-box, and that landed her in conflict with other women. Rose wasn't accustomed to such behaviour; she normally kept close to Diane and the family, and also only had a handful of friends.

One day Rose, was assisting in the shop that same week that she had made up her mind to leave, when a man came in looking like he'd won the lottery.

"Hello" he said

Hello," Rose responded, without paying much attention to the man;, he seemed chatty and it was important to be polite to the customers.

"What are you doing in a place like this?" and at that, instantly Rose realized that he was familiar with the owner. She paused, observing his expression, then said, "what do you mean by that?".

He didn't hold back with his declarations about her, this was the icing on the cake for Rose, considering her own doubts about her employer. 'Well, maybe this is the push I was waiting for!' she thought, trying to find some consolation. He came back in the evening to see Rose, who felt uncomfortable about the idea because she wasn't expecting him to return so quickly. He waited until her shift was over, introduced himself to her as Dave, and then said he was going to accompany her to the bus stop. Rose was new to the area and he looked respectable enough. When Rose got home, Kevin was there waiting for her. Kevin was Maria's oldest son. After he left home he had shared with Rose and her family as a child, he went back to his mother's to live but things didn't turn out so well. Rose knew him; they had grown up together and when he explained what had happened, she was happy to have him stay. The room was a sizable one, so she placed another bed of smaller size there for him. Rose believed that family was everything, and you should be there when they needed you most. Even though Rose had fled home years before, Kevin was close like a brother.

When Rose went back to work the following day, she had one more month to feed. Things went on as usual that day but Rose couldn't wait for her shift to be over so she could get home to her son and nephew. Dave came by before she left.

"I see you're making this a habit," said Rose, who wasn't really interested in him seeing as Calvin had turned out to be such a sour grape. But Dave didn't mind, and he continued to follow her every evening to the bus stop, and eventually it became a regular thing. She didn't leave the job as she had hoped, instead she stayed on for few more months. It was better to have half a loaf of bread than nothing at all. In Jamaica children start basic school from age three to five and begin primary school at the age of six. Rose never forgot that day in September, 1998. Neil was now three years old and was just starting infant school. On his first day that Rose took him he cried like the world was coming to an end, and as a mother she was reluctant leaving him. His face turned pink, and she felt heartbroken, but the teachers were kind and gentle towards him. One held him in her arms, reassuring Rose that he would be fine. She went home wondering, how he'd been during his time there. The good thing was it wasn't for the entire day. By twelve o clock, Rose was getting ready to retrieve him, and when she got there Neil, ran to meet her. The teacher spoke of his progress throughout the day; he did cry a lot, however, he had fallen asleep in the process and when he awoke he seemed calmer. Diane took him the day after, since Rose had to go into work, and for the entire day she was worried about her son., she called Diane's mobile to find out how it went with Neil. To her surprise, he only cried for a short time, and Diane had stayed with him until he was settled down.

Mobile phones had taken a turn for the better, and almost anyone was able to purchase one, if they desired to do so. Some had no cameras, or even an internet connection. Willy had one, but not everyone from Rose community could afford to buy one. Some families and friends were going on a trip and he rang Rose before they set out. "Sis I need you to do me a favour," said Willy.

"Oh yeah, what do you need" Rose replied.

What he said after was so funny, and Rose laughed so hard, but who wouldn't under the circumstances. "In the next ten minutes, please ring my phone," was the strange request.

Rose thought,

"Why?" she asked him puzzled

"I need the passengers in the bus to know that I've got a phone." Several months passed, and Dave was still pursuing Rose. He showed some interest in meeting her son, and she wasn't sure how she felt about this as she was very protective, like aa lioness with her cub; he was walking on sacred ground and had better take care. It took her a long time before she finally did introduce him to Neil and Rose found that she did grow to care about him, not in the way she had once loved Calvin, her son's father, but who had now fallen into disrepute. Dave was helpful, a bit of a jack of all trades, and could do a little of everything. Apparently, Kevin and Dave got on to a certain extent, and he got a job for him. Rose was content with how things were progressing; after all, it been a long time coming. Subsequently

Rose fell pregnant, and she wasn't jumping over the moon about it. Everything now hung on his action when she told him the news, and how he responded. She already had a plan depending on the consequences. To Rose astonishment, he was overjoyed, like a child on Christmas morning. She felt relieved, but it was still a burden. Mr Gus, the old man who owned the yard really cared for Rose, so when she approached him about building a hair salon in the yard, he agreed straight away. Dave gathered all the materials and got down to business and in a few days Rose's hair salon was ready. He had a good attitude towards Rose; the heart can`t lie, no matter how hard you try, and she couldn't help but feel anxious. There was something offbeat, it was all just too good to be true. He was trying too hard for everyone to like him and that came off as seeming too desperate. Rose thought that maybe, she was overthinking the situation, but they had so little in common. Her friend Nada had some issues and needed help, he was being impolite and unfriendly towards her and Rose was furious with him. She warned him that Nada had always got her back, when she was broken, going through some troublesome times, and he needed to step back.

Rose was getting more clients now. The salon was small but got the job done, and she felt content knowing that her struggles were now at a moderate level. Her nephew had a job going, it didn't pay a great deal, but he seemed to be doing well. After a time, Rose went to the landlord asking for his permission for Kevin to build a home of his own. He required his own private space, and the landlord agreed that he could build on the land. He brought the materials, and designed and constructed his single room close to Rose's place, almost like an extension built onto the side. Everyone was living in harmony, sharing what they had with each other. Rose was smart when it came to increasing her earnings. Having a partner is mostly a Caribbean culture, but is also practice by other countries. where individuals come together to save their money on a monthly basic. One person is responsible for collecting all the cash and that person is called the banker. At the end of each month, one person would receive a lump sum until it complete.. Rose normally put her money in the bank; she always believed it was important to put away something for a rainy day, however little.

Neil became more attached to her, he was sensitive boy, and his mother made sure that he was well cared but for having another wasn't an easy responsibility, and on one or two days, her emotions would sneak up on her. Dave was adjusting comfortably, while Rose felt inadequate. In as much as he was doing his best, her instincts about him were filled with inconsistences; some of his faults were hard to ignore, they were too blatant. Rose learnt to guard her emotions and promised herself no one would manipulate her trust again; she shielded her heart like she was the Lone Ranger. Dave was excited at how things were going. He already had a daughter from his previous relationship and she was already a teenager when Rose met her. They got on fairly well, and sometimes she came to visit Rose on her own. Rose always made sure that Dave's daughter was comfortable and content. He introduced Rose to his family, who accepted her wholeheartedly. She liked them and they, in turn, reciprocated the feeling. His mother was a jolly woman and a free spirt indeed who lived with her daughters in their family home where Rose would sometimes go to visit them.

Dave lived on his own in a shared rental where he occupied one room. Rose preferred it that way, even though he spend much of his time at hers, and occasionally when she needed a break from the community, she would go around to his place. During Rose's pregnancy her feeling changed towards him, and unfortunately not in a pleasant way. She was easily irritated by his comments and the things that he sometimes did; he seemed to have a knack of rubbing her up the wrong way. Rose didn't appreciate that. He liked attention and approval from others and Rose noticed this about him. She, however, she was a more private person and disliked attention. She always believed that the less people know about your affairs, the better it was. Rose realised that their relationship was somehow dismal, and for her part, it wasn't anything that he did, but she just couldn't shake that feeling that there was something off about it all. However, in other ways she was doing much better; her salon was doing well and the customers were satisfied with her work as usual.

Willy came to visit her once. It was the first time he'd travelled to such an area of Kingston, and his expression when he arrived was one of astonishment. He looked around the old wooden room, and although he didn't say much but you could see he was scrutinizing the place. But they were happy and delighted to see each other; Rose hadn't seen her brother in years. They were both neat to tears, their emotions were running so high.

"This place looks daunting," he uttered, moving towards the back doors of the room. He stared across the tall zinc fence that separated the two communities from each other.

"Don't worry, it's not as bad as it seems. Everyone knows each other, some are even more frightened than you are, and they do their best to get by".

" Totally Sis, I believe you," Willy gazed at Rose who was smiling awkwardly at him. The day went by pleasantly as they laughed and chatted away. She cooked so that he could eat something before he left, and in the evening Dave came to the house, shouting Rose's name before he entered the room. She just looked right through him, without answering. As he came inside her home, he saw a man sitting on the bed.

"Good evening," he greeted them looking as curious as a cat that had been caught stealing the cream.

"This is my brother, Willy", Rose said to him as she gave him a warning look that was a signal to say, don't discredit yourself. Behave. He had a way of over-talking himself; Rose often thought he was going to talk himself to death, he just never seemed to shut up. Willy wasn't much of a talker, and just sat there smiling like a sunflower. It was now almost seven o clock in the evening and Maria's husband was there, ready to pick Willy up and take him back to the country with him. It saddened her to see him go, and Rose promised that she would come and see the family soon.

Willy was gone, and Rose felt empty, lonely, and filled with despair. After waving her brother goodbye she walked slowly back to her room, her place of solitude. Little Neil came into the room with Diane, and his face lit up the room as he went and cuddled up in his mother's arms. Rose hugged him tightly, kissing him on his cheek, and he kept laughing away as she tickled him. Dave was off on his endless chit-chat again, emphasising how excited he was at meeting Willy. She kept thinking to herself 'oh, my goodness you can surely yap.

A week later she went into labour, and had another son. She named him Sam, and he was such a beautiful boy, although he looked more like his dad than her. She loved hi, with everything she had. Dave was over the moon; he was supportive and helpful more than ever. Rose wasn't alone anymore with the responsibly of been single mother; someone else was there to carry the load with her. Rose was embracing motherhood, but she remained living in her own home; she had no intention of moving in with Dave, that wasn't a part of her ambitions. A year more passed, and things were going fine. Sam and Neil were inseparable, like a couple of swans. Sam would follow Neil everywhere he went. Diane and the others were assisting Rose however they could. Neil's father never returned to see him, but Rose had embraced that a long time ago; she sometimes wondered, and wished things had turn out differently, but maybe it had all been for the best. Sam's father was always there for him, and Rose didn't want Neil to feel left out so she constantly made sure he felt safe and loved.

Rose's sister Jenna lived in Kingston for a short while, although her community was nothing like the one Rose lived in; she was able to stroll in the streets at any given time of the day without fear. Rose was exceptional relieved, she couldn't have handled the strain of her living in conditions such as her own, that would have been a sin of its own. To have someone so close from home was such a comfort, Rose felt that perhaps the gods were finally listening at last. Even if it was for a short time it was alright, and Rose was thankful. She would sometimes go to see Jenna in the city. Before Sam was born, Rose and Neil used to go and spend the weekends at hers, and Rose had found so much solace then; some her happiest memories were of those times. A few months later Jenna went to live at Maria's place but that was only for a brief time, too, and eventually she emigrated to England. Rose felt very lonely after she'd gone, but was ecstatic for her. The opportunity had presented itself and she took it. It was the first such opportunity any of them had had since Rose's brother had travelled to the USA on his farm working programme when he was very young, Unfortunately for him he'd had to return home, and his feet has never touched foreign soil again. This was a remarkable moment; everyone

one was very proud that things had worked out so well for Jenna. It was like a silver lining had now appeared. Years before Rose's dad had beseeched his aunt to help one of his children, the answer that he got was totally dishonourable, but now it was all working out. To be the only immediate family member living overseas had its ups and downs, But Jenna kept in touch with everyone, giving whenever she could, and Rose was no exception.

The surrounding area where Rose lived continued on in its predictable way; the gangs were always up to no good, one person would annoy someone from another group; most of the time it was a prolonged conflict that never seemed to end. Curfews were imposed to keep the peace, and there were armed soldiers on patrol, their presence was petrifying. Often gang members were murdered, their opponents, sneaking up on them when they least expected it. The results of the fatalities meant grief-stricken families. Rose's community remained a getaway for their preposterous behaviour, as they ran through like wild animals. She sat on the porch of her old house, that she had lived in for years, staring down at the red dirt, scattered across the yard. Rose was able to view most of the surrounding area, and could see people moving around relentlessly, seemly disheartened. God forbid if one of these days there's a shootout between rival gangs running through. Then how many innocent lives would be destroyed? "Rose felt the very anxious, chills running down her neck as she suddenly realised how exposed they were. It was Rose biggest fear letting her children grow up in such a deplorable and violence place. These evil people were fearlessly walking the streets, so boldly, with no consideration for their fellow human beings. What life could her children have? Rose searched for diligently for answers, but instead, there were more question than answers, and that was becoming a burden.

The pressure was piling on, and everyone was sacred of what their future would be. Crime rates were on the rise, and people were desperate for change and a new beginning. Individuals who struggled throughout their lives were now trying to leave. It was a massive sacrifice, and something that Rose hadn't seen coming; her people were actually fleeing. The community was becoming more intense to live in, as the residents started moving out. Some emigrated to either America or England; their children needed stability and freedom from the constant, crime and murder in the capital. Nada too had left for England; she was invited by her cousin, and was very excited to be able to go. For years Nada and Rose had talked about how one day they would leave. A few days before she travelled, everything was moving at full speed. She promised Rose that she wouldn't forget her, and so she never did. But the feuds between gangs were becoming too many, and a new era was coming; it was one of great condemnation.

It was raining heavily, as the wind threw the rain onto the narrow porch of the house that Rose called home. She was sitting inside her abode attending to her own business, and was watching the rain drops with her oldest Neil, who was fascinated by its texture. The front entrance door was open, giving a view of the outdoors. Sam was having a nap like any other day, but this one encompassed an unnerving encounter, one that left Rose more troubled than ever. A man was coming up the grey hash colour stairs to her house,. He was smiling, like he knew her, as he walked towards the open door. He was attired all in black, which made him look quite sinister. Rose saw the dark object that he carried in one hand. 'Oh my god! was her first thought,' gazing down at her son and pulling him closer to her. She half recognised his face but still had no idea who he was; when she worked at Ms Peg's she met a few characters who came there to purchase their meals on a daily basis. He called her name.

"Rose" he shouted, and she walked awkwardly towards him; she didn't want to seem intimidated. He suddenly stopped on the second stair; as she approaches him, he raised the hand that had the now visible object – it was a firearm.

"How did you know I lived here?" Rose asked him nervously.

"I didn't know. I was just passing and saw it was you."

She couldn't understand his purpose. Why was he here.

"Do you a plastics bag?" he asked.

Although it was pouring with rain Rose, felt her body was on fire, but she managed to respond, with a yes.

"Stop looking so worried Rose. I`m not here to hurt you. I just need you to tie a bag around this".

She thought that maybe, he was joking. Her son was standing close enough that he was able to see and hear everything.

" I`ll do it, mom" Neil said, gazing at the man's hand.

" No, no, that's alright. I'll do it dear," she said as she gently pulled him away towards the opened door. Rose's knees felt weak but she reasoned that if he had come here to murder her, he would`ve done so already! she tried to come through with some logical explanation in her mind. There wasn't time to analysis the situation as was her custom; the man was still standing there, awaiting his request. Rose quickly glanced around the room looking for a plastic bag, and fortunately she saw a few neatly tucked away, on the wooden table that stood in a corner of the room by the stove. She grabbed the bags from the table and walked speedily towards, the man now standing on the grounds, he lifted his arm that held the weapon. "Please could you tie it for me "he gestured, and Rose trembled with fear, but did it without saying a single word. He took the other bag from her.

"Respect, pretty woman," he said and with that he was off, he was gone. For a moment, it felt unreal like it didn't happen. This wasn't something that she expected would be possible, especially in the middle of the afternoon. Now she started to anticipate all the what ifs! And what nots! Even though time passed, it kept replaying in her mind, like a scratched record, for many days afterwards.

She went inside and closed the door slowly behind her, with nothing but fear and dismay in her heart. 'I wonder if someone were following him, what would've occur? Maybe we would all have been killed. My children are my life. If anything should befall them, I don't know what I would do.' Throwing her hands up in the air, she looked around. "Neil, come watch some TV," she said, and used the remote to search for his favourite cartoon. Sam was now awake, and she made him a bottle as she could see the poor boy was hungry. He, too, was enjoying the entertainment on the television, and luckily Rose had prepared the meal earlier during the day; if not she wouldn't have had the strength to do it now. Rose dished out her son's dinner. She had no dinner table – she couldn't afford one and even if she had wanted one the room was way too small to accommodate such luxury. She pulled out one of his old blankets, spread it on the floor where Neil sat to eat his dinner. There was a tiny bowl, also, for Sam who sat with his older brother. She became worried for the rest of the day and for weeks afterwards; the endurance of her problem had just begun.

Nada was settling nicely in England, was living with her cousin until she moved to stay at her sister's, and occasionally she would call Rose, and chat about how she was settling in to her new place. Her children had been left in the care of their fathers. It wasn't all glitter; the expectation and responsibilities of home were intensifying. No matter what, everyone was more or less the same, having low paid jobs and living in shabby conditions, and those who got the opportunity to make a better life for themselves were now portrayed as braggers. 'How contrary,', thought Rose; she would never understand the mentality of her surrounding neighbours who were too stuck in their ways. Some surmised that once an individual emigrated ,they expected them to support everyone financially, without not bothering to think about that person's own wellbeing and ability to survive. If you weren't able to give, their remarks and criticism were cold. Their view about neighbours was shameless; Rose heard several unkind words spoken, and she believed people were just green with envy.

Rose knew that she had to leave. If she remained here the life that she hoped to give her children would be doomed. The only person who could help her was her sister Jenna. Rose decided to tell Kevin about her plans for leaving. Kevin was excited about Rose's idea, but first she needed to speak with Jenna, to know if she was able to help. She did mention it to Diane also, but asked her not to say anything until she was sure.

Rose spoke to Dave about her concerns; his community wasn't any better, and in some ways could be deemed worse. More people were murdered in that period than Rose could ever have anticipated, and she was worried about leaving Kevin but Diane and the family, would be there for him, as they had been for Rose. To leave for a more suitable life required sacrifices, like saving every last penny, but Rose's motivation was her children, and she was determined to provide that for them.

It was now two years since her sister had emigrated to England, and she had become one of the main backbones of the family. Even when she was unable to bestow upon those who asked for financial help, she would promise for another time. Due to her kindness, some family members took to taking advantage of her, and she knew that, but still pressed on like a trooper. Rose wasn't pleased, but regrettably it wasn't her call, sand he had to respect Jenna's choice. Del was still living at Maria house, and she was now designing and making people's clothing, Del was truly gifted with her scissor fingers, and it was amazing the things that's she could do; top of the chart jobs. She never did really drop by, but they spoke all the time on their mobiles, calling as much as they could. She had a son who was only a month older than Sam. Although Del and had gone through some difficult times, her fighting spirit gave her the determination to endure the hardest of times. She worked hard to support her son even though her health wasn't of the best ever since they were children. Del went back home, on and off, to take a break. They stayed in touch, as much as life permitted them to, considering both of them were battling demons not of their own making; how perverse life can be, when you least expect it. Everything appeared to be degenerating, the community wasn't improving, the residents were desperate, and the poor were still poorer than ever.

CHAPTER 10
A TRIP TO THE FOREIGN LAND

Rose was accustomed to talking things over with herself, speaking out loud and to her inner consciousness until it all made sense. 'I need to asked Jenna for help, otherwise under no circumstance will I ever be able to leave this place. She spoke with Kevin about the matter, who reckoned it was a brilliant idea. It took her a while to gather her courage to ask her sister, and meanwhile Rose had other issues that were weighing enormously on her mind. She had to find someone trustworthy enough to leave her children with, and people's attitude changed when it involves money; she was at a crossroads without knowing which direction to take. Stability and safety were top of her list, but there were many other things just as important. Eventually it was time; the night before Rose was going to speak to her sister she was unable to sleep; her thoughts were getting the better of her. If Jenna wasn't in a position to be able to help, it would be sad to hear indeed, but her sister was one of the most honourable people she knew. Whatever the answer was, it wouldn't be a lie. It was late, as Rose watched through the tiny cracks that stood alongside her bed, and stared into the darkness ,thinking about its mystery outside. She hoped that daylight would appear swoon; that would be the breaking of a new day for her.

Eventually, the outside world became alive; insects crawling, dogs barking and oh, yes, people moving about like they`d been deprived of their slumber. To Rose, it was obvious how burdened they were. Rose was very observant, and easily caught on to other people's emotions, often ignoring her own. She attended to her two boys, the same routine she`d been doing every day since they were born, and maybe the only thing that kept her sane.' I need to call my sister after midday, Rose thought to herself as she was making herself busy filling in the day till it was time to go over to Diane's house,

" Hi cuz, you ok?" she called as she added more red polish to her steps.

"Yes, I`m OK, can't stay long. I've got some things that need sorting." Diane was taken aback by Rose mood, and so she placed the polish bottle on the narrow step that led to inside her home. "Listen you need to stop worrying. Thing are going to get better," she promised, drying the sweat off her forehead as it ran down into her eyes.

"I know. I'll talk to my sister today, get it over with". When she got back Neil and Sam were still watching cartoons. Before long, her phone rang.

"Hello, Sis! How`s everything going on in foreign parts?" Rose said, sounding jovial. They`d always had a light-hearted conversation together.

"I`m doing good Sis, "

They were both laughing and chatting like there were no one else in the world but the two of them. Subsequently Rose gathered her wits and plucked up the courage to ask her sister for help. She was relieved with the answer she got.

"Sis, I`m here for you, I`ll do my best to help. "

Rose was overwhelmed with gratitude; she could now see a dim of light at the end of the dark tunnel. In a few days Jenna would return with an answer.

Rose was at peace with herself. No matter what the answer was, she would accept it and move on. She believed that what is meant to be will surely manifest itself. Business was getting slow but Roe had been saving for a rainy day, regardless, she had some dollars tucked away. Jenna came back with great news – one that changed Rose and her children's lives forever. Everything was planned accordingly, and she managed to keep it a top secret; Diane and the rest of the family knew but they, too, kept it to themselves. The days and weeks were moving rapidly and when all was secure, Rose decided it was high time she went to see her family in the country, and tell them of her news. Friday morning, Rose and her boys were off to Downtown Kingston, getting the bus to Clarendon, and from there to her sister's place. Then her sister's husband would drive them to her parent's house in the country. Rose was delighted to share her joy. When Jenna left for England years before, almost everyone went to the airport to see her off, and for most of them that was the closest they'd ever seen a plane. Her thoughts and attitude were filled with positivity, nothing was going to ruin her day. By then Granny, Ricky's mother had died and so had his father. Ricky was devastated, but as a grown man you`re not allowed to show your emotions; people would see you as weak.

They`d always travelled on a Sunday morning, even when Rose was living with them. There was less traffic and drivers on the road. This would be the first time her family would be meeting Sam since he was born. They knew of his existence but Rose assumed her mother had not once visited her in Kingston because of fear. Kingston's reputation was scary, and coming from a much more moderate neighbourhood, it would have been like throwing a lamb into a den of wild animals. No wonder people took such a negative view of the place – who could blame them? All aboard the old transit, no one was left behind; the road was tranquil, on one side there was a long and narrow gully, while on the other there were rolling hills. Things that Rose hadn't been aware of before were suddenly visible, and she was asking a lot of questions.

"Oh, my goodness there are so many improvements, houses and business in place that were empty land before," she cried.

"Yes, some of these new properties are return residents, who wanted to come back home," Ricky responded, as the others laugh and chattered away. Rose was cheerful to see her family; it had been such a long while, Willy's wife also had a son, their first., and he was only a year younger than her Neil. The journey was a pleasant one, filled with energy and good vibes for Rose. She had found hope, knowing that a change was coming.

This time they knew that Maria and her household were coming, but not Rose. Beep! Ricky sounded his faithful old transit van's horn, calling the attention of everyone who was present in the house. Dave hadn't come with them, Rose didn't care for him to travel with her, so he remained in Kingston; she hadn't known what to expect, and couldn't cope with the extra stress. Ven's children came through the main front door, their faces full of curiosity.

"Mama," one of them shouted. Rose anticipated her next move as she walked slowly towards the van. There she was in her glory; Rose's mother. She came outside, smiling from cheek to cheek, looking very pleased and greeting everyone enthusiastically. Ricky's daughter had one of Rose's sons in her arms.

"Whose baby is this?" she asked , scrutinising the boy closely with her eyes; she probably thought it was Ricky's grandchild. Sharlene burst out laughing.

"No Ms Jane, he`s not mine."

All the time Rose was still sitting there observing the scene. Then, she came out of the van, and embraced her mother.

"I didn't know you were here. What a surprise," her mother said, holding on to Neil's hand, and assisting him from the vehicle. The others came on the veranda, looking on in amusement as even Rose's dad emerged from the house and was standing there.

He was greeted in a respectable order. They were all excited to see each other, and Rose and her mother proceed towards the veranda where everyone was having a jolly time. It was amazing how connected everyone seemed. Rose's dad appeared to be astonished when he saw her; but his expression had a sense of calmness as he kept continue smiling. While Rose was in Kingston, she knew everything that was happening back here; news spreads like wildfire whether it was good nor bad. So, she was frequently updated on his actions, which were often disruptive, although nothing like they'd been years before. Rose greeted him and he looked at her like he was trying to read her mind.

"How you are doing, my daughter,".

They were already familiar with Neil, Rose's oldest, but he was older since they'd last seen him. Sam was quite big now and was doing most things for himself as a toddler; he was holding on to Rose's dad's hand, like he already realised who he was, gazing upon him with his button eyes. Neil had a less self-assured manner, sticking at his mother's side and didn't want to leave her. He seemed more reconstructed in some odd way, and that was refreshing to see, you could feel the atmosphere of more positive vibes. They chatted and laughed like nothing Rose had experienced at home in ages. During the course of the day she told them that she came to say goodbye, and their reaction was filled with enthusiasm and delight; she had finally made them proud and as she looked around the room, those were her thoughts.

Rose went by Willy's house; he only lived a stone's throw away from the family home where they'd grown up. She walked slowly up the narrow slope that led to his home, shouting Willy and his wife's name out loud. She was standing at the unfinished house, knocking at the wooden door. Willy wasn't home but his wife came out, and you could see her surprise, she and Rose had been friends for years, they'd been more like sisters than anything else. Not long after Willy came back home, he saw the old transit van, so he knew that they were around. Rose told of her plan to leave for England.

"I'm proud of you, Sis. I've always know that you're ambitious," Willy told Rose, shaking his head in approval. The day was going fantastically, and she couldn't have asked for anything else. Rose's parents were happy also, knowing that Jenna wouldn't be alone anymore. Rose was seeing her father in a different way. He didn't say much but she acknowledges his change and so a part of her saw him as the father she had been waiting for all her life. The business he cherished was still progressing, but had less customers than before for whatever reason;, some just chose to shop elsewhere. Nothing about the house had been upgraded; everything remained the same but was painted every Christmas as was their custom. Rose's dad was also better at managing his finances; times were altering, and he had to make decisions.

The sun was now hiding among the clouds, the chill of the evening was the arising, and even the streetlight knew it was time to light up. Rose's dad went into the field and brought back yams and green bananas for them to take back with them. Rose's mother promised to bake a sweet potato pudding before Rose went off travelling and so she did, adding a few other goodies for Jenna. Everyone said their goodbyes. Rose was overwhelmed by their support and in her heart she was content; building bridges with her dad was truly a triumph. She knew that there was more work to do, but at least they had made a start; for now it was enough, 'one day at a time,' Rose thought as she smiled to herself. The process wouldn't be too difficult. The old transit van was ready to leave, and she felt heartbroken; she wasn't sure when they would see each other again. They were all trying to make light of the situation; the journey back seemed shorter than ever. Rose was distracted by the uncertainty that rested on her mind, a foreign country wasn't a bed of roses. Rose had a plan, she hoped to enrol in a nursing school when she got to England, then file for her children to come over, but it wasn't as easy as she thought. Rose was about to find out the hard way.

She wanted her boys to reside in the same place, so that they could grow up together, Maria was willing to keep Neil, and Dave, Sam's dad, believed he was the most suitable candidate for his own son. Rose was disappointed that her children would be separated. It wasn't what she had hoped for but that was her best offer. Rose didn't object to his demand; he was dead keen, but she had doubts about him, he was too much of a free spirit.

"Are you sure that it will be alright keeping our son? When you go into work, what's going to happened to him?" she asked quite reasonably. "I`ll leave him at my mother's," he responded looking sure of himself. Rose stared at him in a serious manner,

"Hmm, please don't make me regret this." It wasn't her intention to judge him; he should be the best person – after all he was his father.

It was now two days before Rose was to leave for England, and Diane accompanied her downtown to purchase the clothing she would need. After they finished, she went home and had her hair done. Rose was excited for a new beginning but also felt terrified of the unknown. The worst thing was leaving the best part of herself behind – her boys. All this time Rose had been staying at her sister's house, as she didn't want to travel from the community where she lived in Kingston; it was better that way. Diane and the family knew this but even that was a secret, and they remained tight-lipped about it. The day had finally arrived. Rose had everything in place for her journey; the only that kept her positive was that she was doing this for her children, and that they would join her soon.

Rose held her sons tightly, Neil smiling at her every chance he got, like he knew somehow. She held Sam in one arm while hugging Neil with the other. The old faithful transit, never blundering along the way, was moving at a steady speed; there was laughter, joyfulness and hope among the travellers. Ricky picked Dave up on their way to the airport at Kingston; he greeted everyone who was in the vehicle, and then took Sam from Rose's arms. He was excited for Rose; he probably hoped that one day, he too, would be join her in England. But he was unable to conceal his disheartened expression from them as he played with his son throughout the journey. They didn't discuss much about her leaving around Neil, as they were worried about his reaction. The closer Rose came to the airport, the more nervous she became,. It should have been a happy occasion, but there was nothing but high emotions put on hold. She was more troubled about her children, and the effect of her not been there would have on them. The airport building was gigantic, spreading over many acres of land, and they could see aeroplanes flying into the skies like giant bids made of metal: some seemed nearer than others. There were guards everywhere, travellers pulling their suitcases along, more like a marketplace but in a different order. Ricky found a parking place, then they all got out. Rose looked around with amusement and excitement. None of them had travelled before, so she was inclined to ask question as she went along; she had her suitcase and a pully bag, and eventually she went inside to check in her luggage.

Rose went back outside to be with her family until she was ready to embark on her journey, and they spent much of the time that remained, wondering what the flight will be like, 'on that big ol' iron bird?' The sea breeze blew, sending chills down her arms. It was now time to go back into the airport terminal, so everyone said their goodbyes. Maria took Neil away; he was inconsolable and his screams melted Rose's heart. Sam didn't seem to mind much. He had his dad with him, who kept him distracted, he was so young that they weren't sure that he understood. Rose pulled her brown pully bag behind her and as she went through checkout, she glanced behind her. Everyone was waving excitedly. Rose went through the double doors, then was ushered away into a tiny room; her instinct told her that something wasn't right. Not knowing was the worst, her observation led her to wonder as to what she had done, having no idea what would happen next. As she entered the narrow door, she saw a black woman who was so tall she almost looked like a giraffe in comparison to Rose . She had an odd smile on her face, and was wearing a set of disposable gloves.

"Could you pull your pants down," she said.

"Excuse me" Rose answered awkwardly; the woman was trying to pretend that it was normal procedure. Rose felt demoralized even though she didn't touch her, but it didn't make any difference.

"What were you looking for," Rose asked the woman, who pretended not to hear her, then she said in a husky man's voice

"Oh you can go now," as she opened the door. She had heard stories of things like this happening but never knew that she, too, would fall prey of such malarkey. 'How dare she?', Rose questions herself. The alarmingly encounter triggered her mind into pure doubt. If they knew her, they wouldn't have such a horrible imagination. Her attire was casual but perhaps not enough, for them. Rose wasn't smiling anymore; all her emotions had dried up. By then people were boarding their flight, but she did manage to catch up with the crowd. Everyone seemed enthusiastic, you could tell by their expression. They were a mixture of people, some were returning home from holiday, others visiting. Rose seat number placed her at the window and she gazed outside, thinking of what she had left behind; maybe what had just happened was God punishing her for leaving her family. She felt empty and confused. A well-dressed woman sat beside her in the next seat; she seemed like someone who had travelled many time s before.

"Hello," she greeted Rose.

"Hmm, hi," Rose managed to whisper. The woman was friendly, a bit of a show-off but she didn't shout her mouth for the entire trip.

Can tell it's your first time," she said conclusively."

"How did you know that," Rose replied, uncomfortably. By the time she finished explaining her theory, Rose was convinced she was right; obviously she wasn't dressed for the weather that awaited her.

The flight was a long one. 'Oh my God,' Rose thought. No one informed her of what to expect, coming from a tropical country; she had no conception of what it would be like. Rose began to recall that most of the people that were at the airport, and now passengers on the plane, were dressed for a colder temperature. The woman sitting beside her, had a winter jacket on; Rose had never seen a winter jacket before, that was the first time. She pretended to fall asleep and that was when the woman finally went quiet. Rose was awakened by cold air and a stuffy nose, and she wrapped herself in a blanket that was provided, within the space she occupied inside the plane.

As she looked through the window, she noticed how dark and thick the clouds were getting, and Rose couldn't erase that awful picture of what had happened back at the airport from her mind. How people could be judged so easily, without the facts, because of what someone else thought about them. That was unacceptable; such betrayal was cold and brutal, something like that you never forget. Lingering on those ghastly moments Rose's thoughts were becoming alive. She just stared into space, hoping she could disappear.

"We're almost there," the woman spoke, tapping Rose lightly on her shoulder.

" Yeah," Rose nodded her head. She was beginning to wonder if she had made the right choice by going to England; she felt overwhelmed, could hear her son screams as the echo`s kept rewinding, over and over in her mind.

The sky was pitch black; you couldn't see much if it was poking you in the eyes. The woman was watching a tiny screen in front of her, as Rose's heart suddenly leapt, and she wasn't sure how to feel. She feared the unknown, her confidence was knocked out completely, and Rose was hanging on by a straw, gradually slipping away. The motion of the plane was different now, it felt weird, and after a while there were lights in the far distance, as the clouds slowly vanished. Her only comfort was that she would be seeing her sister who she hadn't seen for years. Such a reunion! 'God give me strength,' she kept repeating to herself. The lights were getting closer, and now she could see houses in the far distance. It looked like it was cold and foggy, like nothing Rose had ever seen before. After a while the plane landed. The airport was massive, and everything looked so different, everyone was moving like they'd done this lots of times before, except for her and a few other people who from their reactions, she guessed it was their first time, too. She wasn't in any hurry; whatever was out there wasn't going anywhere. Eventually she manged to make it outside, dragging her pully bag with her, feeling like a lost soul. The temperature was shocking, like she was in a huge freezer.

"Oh, if only I'd taken the blanket with me!" The other passengers from the flight were wearing their warm jackets, even the woman that had sat beside her on the plane. By this time, the woman was long gone, though, and the lines were stretching endlessly. Rose felt like a fish in deep water. Rose approached the tall, skinny white man at the desk, and she knew straight away that again there would be significant inconsistencies. The man at the desk had piercing blue eyes, and narrow check bones, and he was asking Rose the most unusual questions, as if he already knew what had transpired earlier, before she got on the plane. This was no coincidence; they`re working together, she thought. The waiting was extensive and painful. 'What have I done to deserve this torment?' she thought, holding the tears back. In as much as Rose wanted to be in England, in that moment she desired to leave. Suddenly the nerves in her body felt expired, having little or no energy left to cope. 'Is this the price of seeking a new life?' Rose had never done anything illegal in her life, yet the curse of a million slaves had haunted her very soul. Her thoughts were poison, with a confusion of questions that didn't seem relevant, but she knew what they were insinuating, and she felt less than a human being. He was manipulative and cunning, but his efforts were in vain. The man walked away saying he was going to speak to another colleague; He appeared defeated. Rose sat on a chair watching their every move, like a hawk hunting its prey.

He came back, charging in like an old stallion, and there was nothing left for them to do to Rose; her energy was being consumed by their deadly plot, but even then she kept defending her good name. That day Jenna, with her friend, was at the airport to pick Rose up but the never saw her; she waited for hours and eventually they had to go back home without her. Rose was placed in a room filled with what seemed like unscrupulous characters; at that point it didn't matter who was guilty, or innocent; no one was safe. Everyone was apprehensive, not sure about the outcome of their fate. Rose felt destroyed, in her country of origin at least she had her family, but being in a strange land it felt like torture. The fact that she was squeaky clean gave her a little hope that maybe in the end they would realise how wrong the we`re about her. It was now late evening and darkness was all around, as she looked through a broad transparent, window that was secured with metals bars. Rose kept to herself, she didn't speak a word, just listen intently. Returning would be humiliating; of all those who'd left before, no one had been sent back in such a shameful manner. She was puzzled and perplexed. Her hopefulness for a better future for her children was sliding away, and she wasn't sure what was going to transpire, but regardless, in a small fraction of her heart she felt a droplet of faith.

Roll call as the names were selected, one by one the smiles of the chosen, their faces were a proof of their freedom and reunion with loved ones. Rose waited and waited, until the room was almost empty. With a distressing sigh she was yet again left disappointed. 'Lord why me? Have I done something that displeases you? Please forgive my selfishness, but if you ever love me as you declare, help me prove my innocence'. A short impeccably dressed woman came to the door, shooing everyone out of the room. They walked behind her through a long and narrow corridor, and at the end a van was waiting to carry them away. This was shocking, and Rose was praying for a miracle. The driver didn't seem friendly but was polite in a weird way. He drove for a while, and eventually he came to the halt. To some this was familiar, but Rose had no idea where she was. Another passenger from the vehicle saw Rose suffering, and she introduced herself; she was kind and cheerful. She explained to Rose that the building, was a place where most of those who entered were likely to be returned to their country.

The building was remoted and isolated, and its intimidating energy felt alive. Inside Rose observed that most of the staff were attired in uniform. Her heart sunk deeper into despair. but it was like a prison designed to manipulate one's situation. The woman had no desire, to contest their decision whatever; she was ready to clear out, she told Rose.

"I was here few year ago, but I got home sick, so I went back home." she continued, her voice filled with contentment. "Oh, really, Rose replied, feeling rather defeated. She didn't have the strength to kept talking. Her brain felt paralyzed, everything seemed to be processing slower than ever. They were placed in a large room where everyone could see each other, some were devastated, others were conversing using the moment to meet new acquaintances. Rose was in a distraught mood, and didn't care much about socialising. By then it was clear to her sister that something horrible had happened. There were phones available for those who needed to use them. Rose had her sisters' number in her bag So she decided to call her, informing her of the agonising situation she was facing. Jenna wept bitterly, having no solution for Rose's predicament.

"Hmm, yeah, so maybe tomorrow I'll return home Sis," she said choking back the tears.

"Don't give up. God works in mysterious ways," her sister answered. After a few minutes they said their goodbyes.

The night went by quickly, leaving Rose no room for sleep as she watched throughout until daybreak. It was time for them to embark on the unknown. At that point Rose wasn't sure of the outcome, it was out of her hands. The vehicles were waiting on the premises, and as Rose mounted into the transport she felt hopeless. The driver wasn't the same man, but that was of little importance to her. As the bus started to move, it was heading off in the same direction it had come from the previous night; everything looked the same except now it was daylight. A duplication of events was occurring. Rose wore the same clothing she'd worn since she arrived. It was now almost three days, taking into consideration the time difference between the two countries, and the night she had slept at the centre. Her body felt aged beyond her years and Rose, just wanted to curled up in a box . Many had no chance of intervention, as they were taken straight away to board a flight to return home; even her new comrade was gone. For Rose, and a few others, the will of God was still working on their behalf. Surely she had no fight remaining in her; they took all that away. Walking towards hope she felt empty of something that she desired and had so much enthusiasm for.

"Come this way please," ordered a woman immigration officer. Rose rubbed her nose, forcing a smile. The night before Rose had met a young black woman at the holding centre, who was being returned to Jamaica, although she didn't want to go. However, she was friendly and kind towards Rose and because it was cold she gave Rose a blue cardigan. Now, sitting with the immigration officer inside the room, Rose was grateful for the cardigan, as it was really chilly .

"Please take a seat," the woman said, pointing to a chair on the other side of the wooden desk. She tossed her head back as if she was commanding it to stay in one place, and she examined the file that sat on table in front of her.

"Would you like a cup of tea?" she asked, tapping her black fountain pen against the desk.

"Yes please," Rose said glancing at her briefly.

" There. Help yourself," she had a calmness to her voice that comforted Rose's mind after her days of torment. Rose wasn't familiar with, nor had seen such teapot before; it kept the water hot throughout the day. She got up from her chair and walked slowly towards the table. Rose took a cup from a pack and placed it on the table adding a teabag, picking up the kettle nervously she made herself a cup of tea. She sipped the hot tea and it almost burned her lips. 'Why is she being so kind to me,' Rose wondered. She gazed across the room; there were several other people moving about, like they had important business, and you could tell they worked there. After sitting there for almost half an hour, she spoke respectfully and politely as if she was taught to do so.

"Conclusively, we`ve come to a decision." Rose's thought her heart would suddenly stop beating

It's OK. Don't look so scared," the woman was smiling between the words, "you're free to go visit your family."

"Excuse me?", Rose asked her, as she thought that she wasn't hearing correctly.

"Please do enjoy your stay here," the woman continued.

Rose was beside herself with joy, as the woman explained to her where to go to collect her belongings.

"Thank you," Rose said to her gracefully, her hopes just starting to re-emerge again. She walked out of the office, and it was like the burden of the world had lift off her entire body. All this time Rose's sister had probably thought she was on the plane, returning home. Rose needed to call her, to inform her of the excellent news. She found a payphone but had no idea how to operate it. A kind man saw her and asked if she was alright. She explained that she needed to use the phone, and the man placed some coins in the box and dialled the number for her.

"Hello," her sister answered.

"Sis it's me, come get me at the airport. It was a mixture of shock and astonishment.

"Oh, yes. We'll be there as soon as we can." Jenna didn't living nearby so give and take it would be another two hours before she arrived. She told Rose where to wait, and then Rose went to get her suitcase; It looked a bit damaged but was in one piece. Her body ached all over, the discomfort was throbbing, and Rose felt sadness within her soul,; her energy was low even though she was beginning to see a glimmer of light. She waited inside the large building that, once kept her prisoner. She felt cold and hungry, and at one moment Rose believed that she was hallucinating because she thought that she saw her mother calling her. She added on her mask, the one that kept her smiling.

CHAPTER 11

THE BEGINING AND THE END

Rose had found the whole experience very challenging for her, making situation more awful. Eager to leave the building but unable to do so because the vehicle hadn't arrived yet. She pulled up the zipper of the cardigan to stay warm but even with a thousand layers, underneath her body wasn't responding. People were leaving frequently going to and fro, and she anxiously checked the time with a big grey clock on display. She had another fifteen minutes before her sister would arrive, so she moved closer to the entrance Rose noticed the streetlights were already on so it must be night-time. The weather was like nothing she had felt in her lifetime, the cold penetrating through her weak and tired bones. It was taking much longer than anticipated, but Rose knew that her sister would come. "Rose," a voice shouted out to her, and just a few metres away was her sister, in a green car driven by a friend. The man came out and took the suitcase from Rose; he told her to go sit in the car where Jenna was, with the windows half rolled down. The reunion was spectacular, and at last Rose felt a sense of peace. That was truly a significant moment, one that she would always remember.

They chatted over the entire length of their journey. Jenna was just as she imagined, beautiful as the morning glory; it reminded Rose of when they were children. She seemed paler due to the weather, Her friend joined in the conversation now and again but he wasn't much of a talker. However, he was tall, good-looking guy, and his presence held a certain mystery about him. All the road signs and designs appeared to be like those back home, it was like a Deja vu, except it wasn't. They drove on and stopped at a fish and chips shop; Rose hadn't seen one before. This was something completely different for Rose; back home they had fast food outlets, but nothing to this extent, where it was if there was one at every corner. She wasn't in the position to be buying such things, she couldn't afford to, but by then she didn't care as to what she ate. After buying the food from the grocery store, the journey to Jenna's home took just a short time. The building which was in a complex made of bricks, was unique in structure on the outside. The windows were rather clear and transparent, as if it was inviting you in; they walked up a flight of stairs that went up to the apartment and Jenna's friend was kind enough to help Rose with her suitcase. There were other people living in the building, and Rose noticed that each door had a number displayed on it. The inside of the flat was warm and homely; Rose's sister showed her the bathroom, where there was a supply of warm water – how original, thought Rose. Back at her parent's house they, too, had a bathroom but the water pressure wasn't strong enough to push through the pipes so, instead, they took their showers in the outside bathroom using a large bath pan, and besides, they had never used warm water.

Rose was longing for a shower; it had been several days.

"Sis something's wrong," Rose said in a strange voice; her jeans hung onto her skin like it didn't want to let go but in a painful way. She sat on the bathroom floor to examine where the shooting pains were coming from. Rose's armpits and feet were covered with large abscesses under her skin.

"Oh my god, I didn't have them," before she said, and straight away she knew. Rose's body had gone through multiple stages of shock and distress for three days, resulting in her infection. She was unable to walk the following day, the abscesses were becoming worse and Jenna didn't know what to do. There appeared to be yellow fluids building up inside so Rose declared that the best thing to do was to squeeze them out. but after several unsuccessful attempts her sister suggested,.

"Let me do it for you, Rose."

"Hmm, I`ll have to prepare my mind for this then," and they both looked at each other, laughing.

"If I don't laugh, I'll be crying, isn't that true Sis?"

"For real," her siter responded.

Jenna knelt ready, pressing against the first abscess, and soon a hideous secretion was flowing out. Rose had stuck a rag inside her mouth, biting on it hard so that she wouldn't scream.

After several attempts to empty the abscesses, victory finally prevailed, leaving weird holes where they had been. Rose, felt relieved, and after a few days she was back to her new self. The home-made food that Rose's mother had given her for Jenna had spoiled. The sweet potato pudding and fried fish. Nothing was saved. "What a waste! I was looking forward to eating the pudding. There's just the tinned products preserved," Jenna, said disappointedly. However, they were delighted to have each other, and Rose could tell that her sister wasn't so lonely anymore; it was like they were always there together. Rose was calling home as often as she could; about three days per week. She enlightened her family about what had happened to her but assured them that Jenna and herself were doing well. During that time, they didn't have their own land line, so had to pay to make calls at the internet shops, which were mostly operated by Somalis .She would try to talk to her children when she called. Neil was missing her terribly and so was Sam. Rose would often cry like her heart would break. Dave and she communicated on a regular basis, but his behaviour was starting to trouble Rose. He was becoming obsessive and manipulative, asking Rose for money when he knew she had no job. Rose was gravely concerned about Sam's wellbeing; his father wasn't living up to his words, and when he went into work, he would drop Sam off at different places.

"Why are you doing that? You told me that your family would help you." Rose asked him. His answer didn't make sense and she was getting frustrated.

In the yard that he originally resided, Dave would also leave their son with his neighbour and his three sons. This was disturbing news for Rose to hear. Often there were horrid stories of people abusing children, and she didn't want her son falling prey to such an ordeal. Diane also informed Rose of another upsetting revelation about Dave; he was behaving indecently, even approaching her inappropriately, and she wasn't amused by him. At the time when Rose emigrated to England, Dave had a job where he was being paid weekly, but his present greediness for cash would lead you to believe otherwise. Jenna, knew the owner of a Caribbean restaurant where they needed someone to assist in the kitchen. The pay wasn't much but was better than having nothing. The days had become weeks and then months and Rose was sending whatever she could, for both children.

It had been almost the end of the year when she arrived. So early the following year, it snowed quite heavily. Luckily Jenna had already prepared for Rose's arrival. Knowing that she was coming for winter, and wouldn't have anything suitable to wear, she bought some winter

clothing for her. Rose had never experienced anything like snow before
. She picked it up off the ground in amusement. They went outside
to romp in it like they children. Jenna rolled the snow into balls and
was throwing them at Rose; it was more fun than she expected. Rose
felt its textures, building angels and a snow man. They went almost
everywhere with each other.

"Sis we`re going to the market, we need items for the house," Jenna
said to Rose as she collected her outdoor clothing. Rose was excited to
go, and was ready and willing.

"Oh yes, it's about time," she replied, laughing. The market was
well-organised and well kept, she could tell the vendors took pride in
their work.

Everyone who had emigrated years before, whether they were
friends, associates or just well-wishers, were getting in touch with Rose.
Jenna wasn't familiar with some of Rose`s acquaintances so they would
travel together regularly. Rose and her sister really connected with each
other, sharing and laughing at the same jokes, having the same history,
and childhood. They would often reminisce about the good old days:
even though they'd had a tough upbringing , it wasn't all so bad, and
they had lots of shared happier memories, too. They would be making
jokes and just being silly; you could often hear their giggling and Rose
they weren't afraid to show their togetherness. They were not so much
just sisters, but best friends as well, relying on each other's truthfulness
and sincerity. Having not lived together for so many years, Rose was
delighted at how well they got on. Nada, her friend from back home,
also got in touch with Rose and they both visited each other. She had
changed in personality, but it wasn't a major thing. Rose felt a little
betrayed by her actions, and they didn't communicate for a while but
Nada wasn't a person to stay bitter. She reached out to Rose, and after

some time they were back on talking terms again, although to be honest things were never really the same.

Rose's first job was through an associate from back home, although they didn't reside in the same community. She was Nada's sister, and their relationship was sometimes odd, but that was their way. She was in the country when Rose came over, and luckily after a few months she returned home. Nada's sister had a job working in the kitchen of a care home. However before leaving, she introduced Rose to the supervisor, and was overjoyed to get the job. Her focus was taking care of her children and this would allow her to do that. 'Oh! Thank you, god, for your blessing,' she rejoiced. The woman was friendly and easy going,

"Can you start tomorrow, dear", she addressed Rose.

"Oh, yes please. That's not a problem."

As soon as Rose left the office she called Jenna.

"Sis, I got the job." Her sister was very happy for her and things went well for a while; Rose was sending money every month for her boys. She was hoping that at some point she could go to college to fulfil her dream of being a nurse. Unfortunately, it kept fading further and further away. It was like catching at straw that was being swept away down the river.

Dave was getting more unpleasant and overpowering; his desire was to come over to England and be with Rose. She wasn't in the position to help him to do so but he didn't seem to care. Maybe for some people it works, but for Rose it was hard, although she had to put on a courageous face as normal. She needed to remove Sam away from Dave but wasn't sure how to accomplish it. He even refused for Sam to spend some time with Diane. Rose was devastated, and what made matters worse was that Dave had made a comment that was disturbing for her, although he had found it entertaining.

"You must be joking, watching inappropriate films with a child," Rose shouted at him. The comment that Sam had made, bearing in mind that he was only a toddler was, for Rose, a danger sign for the future. Her own upbringing had been strict and extremely disciplined. They would never have sat and watched a movie with her parents, where two people were engaging in sexual activities. It was the most uncomfortable feeling; it was just never a thing that they did. Rose realised that maybe she had made a mistake about Dave's fatherly skills, in which he seemed to be completely lacking and that scared the wind out of her.

He laughed but Rose didn't find it funny, and instead she felt angry. He behaved as if she was over-reacting, and it was a natural that this made her more determined than ever to act on her plan to get her son away from his dad. Rose told her sister of the unpleasant event and Jenna wasn't happy about it either.

"He's disruptive. Why does he act like that? He's always calling, complaining about how broke he is, even when you send him cash," she repeated, looking confused.

Hmm yeah, Rose replied. I need to get my son away from him; it's just a matter of time. She sighed!

"I'll discuss this with mama and papa; I know that they won't refuse to help me."

"So how are you going to get him away, Rose?" her sister asked impatiently, as she walked into the kitchen, for a cup of water.

"Not to worry Sis, I got this. Because he finds money so appealing, I'll just give him some. "I'll ask him to send Sam to our parents for the summer holidays."

Jenna burst out laughing, "are you sure that will work?" she said, still chuckling. Rose had to start chuckling then ‑they had to find the funny side to it. The next day Rose called Dave, putting her plan into motion. Just as she predicted, he was enticed by the mentioning of money. Rose arranged that one of her family members would collect her son from Kingston. Rose felt a little compunction about what she was doing, knowing how much Dave love his son but she already convinced herself that this was the right thing to do.

He once told Rose that he had a son that he didn't maintain because of the mom's parents. It made a negative impression on him. She had asked him why and his answer was inconsistent gibberish, almost as if he were proud of himself for abandoning his son. After a time, Rose stopped asking, and obviously he did seem relieved at that, but for her that was a horrible thing to do. Anyway, Sam was now spending some time with Rose's parents, or so Dave thought. As far as Rose knew the grandchildren were treated in a much better way than she and her siblings had been treated. So in sending Sam there, she knew he would be taken care of. Now it was time to convince him that it was the right thing to do to leave Sam there. For him having Sam would connect them together and he knew that the summer holidays were now over.

"When is my son coming home," he demanded, as Rose listened on the other end of the phone. Rose was very calm, and had no intention of raising her tone. She was suddenly reminded him of what he had told her few months prior to that, when he had told her what Sam had said after watching that inappropriate film with his Dad.

"Listen," she said to him, "if I had asked you, to let Sam go to my parents to stay, would you have agreed? The phone line went silent and for a minute Rose, thought he might hang up on her. He then replied, "no I don't think I would.

"Hmm, you can go and see him whenever you want. I'm sorry I had to deceive you like this, but my child comes first. In the end, the matter was settled and merely spoken of. He did visit a few times and then he stopped. The last time he went, he complained that he had no money, so Rose did feel obliged to send him some for the journey. He tried to make her feel guilty, for not helping him emigrated to England, which was inconsiderate of him, knowing that she wasn't in a position to do so. Dave and Rose stayed in touch for a few years and then eventually went their separate ways.

Rose worked in the care home kitchen for nearly a year, and made several attempts to enrol into college, which was disappointing because she didn't have the right paperwork. She felt like a disappointment, feeling sorry for herself. What made matters worse was that Rose, lost her job after a year, when new management took over and regulated their staff. Rose knew she wouldn't be one of the chosen to be kept on, so she took off before been exposed. Neil and Sam were her prime reason for going to England, because she wanted a better life for them. Rose believed herself fortunate, because she was able to support her boys in ways that it wasn't possible if she was still in Jamaica. Rose and her sister were a force, working together, and united they did make a difference by assisting and helping their families. Sam was now living with her, parents, closer to his brother, Neil, but not close enough. Rose would call her children every other day, so that they could remain together, talking about their daily activities and routines. Neil was doing really well in school, always asking a lot of questions.

"Mom, when will I see you?" he would ask every time, his little voice filled with hope.

"Soon dear," she replied, holding back the tears. Rose paused briefly, then she said,

"I love you" to which he replied, "I love you too mummy," and then he was gone to play.

Rose's sister, Maria, told Rose how well he was doing, in school.

"Sis, you should be so proud of herself, I know that you miss him,".

"Yeah, more than you can imagine, but I've something to attended to. Chat soon."

"OK, then, goodbye," and they both hung up the phone.

Sam was mischievous sometimes. Rose's parent used to say,

" he must inherit it from his father's side of the family."

"Mama put him on the phone, please. "Sam could hear Rose's mother calling him, and when he came he was out of breath like he was running for the marathon.

"Hello mummy," he said sounding nervy.

"What's the matter?" she would ask him. "Are you behaving yourself?

"Yes mummy, "Sam would finally respond.

"I love you Sam and please listen to your grandparents," Were Rose's last words as she said, goodbye.

A few years had passed, and Rose made sure to pack a parcel every other year, always making sure that they had clothing and food and on a monthly basis she would send money for them. It was difficult at the time, but Rose kept pushing herself, she wasn't going to add that responsibility on anyone. She made a promise to her boys to take them one day, but that seemed harder by the minute. Sometime Rose felt like the universe was punishing her, it took her a while to accept her situation. She and Jenna were constantly there for each other, knowing that better days would come one day.

After parting ways from her job, it was time to find another one. While Rose had worked at the kitchen, she had met a couple of people that she did their hair for them. Luckily for her, it came in at a time that she needed it the most. Doing her sister hair was another great way of advertising her hand-crafted work. Rose had a high volume of responsibilities which meant sending more money back home. Rose had been saving something away, but that too had come to an end. She sighed!

"Sis don't look so troubled, something will come along soon," Jenna said as the got ready to go to the supermarket. She picked up a note pad and started writing.

"Yeah! I know," Rose said as she sat on a chair tying up her old blue trainers, smiling pleasantly.

"Last week, when I went into the mall, I saw some people signing on individuals for a job," her sister continued.

You serious, Sis. Rose pulled her jacket from behind the door and was ready, as fast as a rocket. "So, you think they`ll be there today?" Rose felt this was a portent of good luck.

"Well who knows? Hopefully we`ll see them," her sister answered, stepping out the doors.

Few moment later they were off. Rose and Jenna chatted for the entire journey, laughing at each other's jokes and whatever seemed funny. They stood at the bus stop waiting for the bus to embark and their quest. After a short while there was the double decker bus coming down the road, towards them.. The first place that they entered was the shopping centre, looking for the helpful organisers. Jenna was leading the way already knew where she saw them before.

"Sis, this is the place," she said seemingly pleased with herself. Two young white women were there writing down names; it was like the first morning of school and teachers were making sure everyone was registered.

"What it is you're after, one asked politely, to which Rose replied, "a hairdressing job please."

"Ok, that can be arranged", and she went on her phone and spoke with someone, her tone sounding very sincere. "Rose, you need to be at this place for nine o'clock, Friday morning," she said as she wrote the details down and handed it to her on a piece of paper.

"Thank you very much. I'll be there," Rose relied, pushing the paper into her bag.

"Also take our number and let us know how it went."

With that she and Jenna were off into the market. They continued with their shopping and then went home, still chatting away. Rose was thankful, there were other jobs available, but if she didn't have the right paperwork, she wasn't bothered, she was too pleased about her day.

It was now the year 2002. Friday morning came at last, and Rose was off. The night before she and her sister went and googled the information about how to arrive at the salon.

"Sis, I seriously wish you could come with me," Rose said, giggling nervously.

"Just make sure that you call me if there's any issues," Jenna responded.

Rose went and caught the bus that took her to her destination. The street was crowded, decorated with clothing shops on both sides of the street, full of colours beyond your wildest dreams and enchanting wedding gowns waiting to be chosen. Rose went into the salon, but it wasn't the right one. However, the owner directed her to the correct one. When she arrived, the owner had just opened.

"Hello, good morning. My name is Rose," but before she could finish her sentence the young women interrupted her.

"Oh yes! I was expecting you," she said, smiling. She appeared to be underfed, overconfident, and arrogant and as Rose looked at her, she went on about her life story in seconds. The hair salon was tiny, but she kept it clean and tidy, hair books with different styles on a table. Another young black woman who seemed to work there, came later.

"You can start tomorrow, Rose," she said.

"OK. Thank you. Nice meeting you," Rose responded as she walked off.

Rose called her sister before she got home, telling her of the day she had, and the impression that the salon owner left on her. They laughed on the phone about the whole thing. The following day Rose went back, her instinct was right, the owner was rude and domineering. She and her partner would even argue in front of her clients, which she didn't find at all practical. The atmosphere was too toxic; Rose wasn't going to be consumed by such negative energy, this was all too familiar. With much pressure, and a commanding approach, the young woman ordered her staff not to take customer's phone numbers – it was strictly forbidden. But Rose didn't have to make inquires for numbers; they were given freely because the customers liked her subtlety and calm nature, not to mention her professionalism. After a month Rose left the salon in search of something else, but she kept in touch with a few of people she met there, and one day as she sat thinking of her next move, she got an unexpected called. At Rose's previous job she had met a well-spoken American black woman. She was deployed in the country with her family, was dark as cocoa and had a gracefulness about her. Sandy was her name, and she had a proposition for Rose, to come and work for her, and she would introduce Rose to a few people. It was a great opportunity for Rose, but the traveling was a problem. It took Rose almost one and a half hours a day for the journey. Sandy was determined to make it work; she had a plan to open a hair salon in the Huntingdon area where there weren't any black salon's around And everyone was traveling to London to get their hair done. She knew that Rose wasn't able to pull that off on her own, so she went and found a second hairstylist from the area.

Things were looking up again for Rose, but even so nothing was ever smooth sailing; there were always hurdles to jump, and often there were falls, but getting up and starting again had become Roses' best friend. Sandy got her salon, Rose was the top stylist, and Lynna, her other employee, specialized in cornrows and plaits. Their venture was a growing business, and it was amazing for Rose to be part of that growing process. Everyone got on well, but the distance was taking its toll on Rose, plus she had other issues of her own that she was coping with. When all was said and done, she had to make a choice, considering that most of her salary went on travelling. She had two sons who were entirely financially dependent on her. It was hard saying goodbye to Sandy and all the people that Rose worked with and admired. She told Sandy of her decision; she was understanding, but it was clear that she was hurting. They remained in contact but never stayed friends. on the other hand Lynna and Rose kept in touch for many years.

Rose and Auston met while she and her sister were out at the mall together, shopping in Stratford. He was trying to find a suitable pair of pants and shirt for an event, he later told Rose. He held the shirt up to his face, looking at it indecisively, and then he placed it back on the rack. Rose was getting some clothing for her children back in her homeland. She wasn't interested in him; she was only curious about his clothing choices. Jenna and Rose had to pass the aisles to get to the men and boys' section. After picking up several other shirts he walked over to Rose and her sister, looking serious. He then introduced himself to them, and said,

"You look familiar, like someone I've met before," directing his attention towards Rose.

"Who me? I don't think so," said Rose looking sideways at her sister. They spoke for a short time, including Jenna in the conversation. He asked Rose for her number and she gave it to him. She could tell that he was older than Rose. The day after he called Rose, but she didn't answer his call. However, that didn't put him off. Auston eventually messaged her to say that he was trying to get her. That's when Rose started accepting his calls. He started picking Rose up from work in his red Vauxhall car. It felt good having someone who listened, and they became close friends. He, too, came from Jamaica and had four sons from a previous relationship. A few years later, they moved in together when Rose fell pregnant.

By this time Rose had three sons instead of two but kept it a secret for a few months before telling her family back home. No one would've imagined such treachery, that's how she felt towards her boys, and Rose couldn't bring herself to tell them. After years of attempting to bring them over, it seemed pointless. Everyone she asked was unable to do anything and unfortunately Rose had no such power of her own to fulfil such a dream.

During that time she communicated with her family constantly, and especially with her children, Neil, was successful with his exams and was now attending high school. Rose was a dedicated mother, who did everything so her children could have a better life than she had. Although she wasn't physically there, she made it her duty to be their support base. Their fathers had been long gone, without glancing behind their ugly heads. It wasn't fair of them, but she never asked them for help. If she had, they wouldn't have done anything, anyway. As Rose lived in a foreign country they believed that she was more than capable of managing on her own. Rose called her dad; his drinking habit was almost a thing of the past. He was a man of truth and fairness, and often saw things from a different perspective, and that made him special to many. When Rose told her papa that she had another son, he was quiet for a brief second. Rose could hear him thinking, but couldn't imagine what his answer would be. He cleared his throat, then he calmly said,

"it's OK my daughter, life has no boundary of perfection, and we`re all humans, I won't judge you."

Not in a thousand years would Rose have believed she could have such a relationship with her father. All that she was able to say as she held back her tears was,

"thank you papa". After that they talked about the weather, and everything that would have seemed irrelevant before, but wasn't so much then. Rose was given the support she needed, by the person from whom she'd least expected it, and that day her situation changed.

CHAPTER 12
WHERE ARE THEY NOW

Rose finally told her boys; Neil was enormously hurt, Sam was excited about having a new brother, so it appeared. It took Neil a while to come to terms with his beloved mother's betrayal. Rose and her sister weren't living together anymore; the home that they`d share was now gone back to its owner, leaving them to go their separate ways. Rose's sister had her share of sinking into deep waters, holding onto straws. Their mental strength was put to the test, but with a strong family base, they came through. Rose and Jenna remained close, supporting each other no matter what the time or the hour of the day. It was the hardest struggles that either of them had to endure in their lifetimes – they named it 'the season of the great depression', and they still reminisce about it even to this day. Finding strength in each other was all they had and so Rose, and her sister survived. As the oldest Rose felt responsible for protecting her sister. The importance of their spirituality was another prospect that kept them convinced that a better future was coming, and so eventually that day did come, not straight away, but it did. During this time Rose, was now working from home, making just enough to support her boys and help with whatever bills she could. Rose met some awesome people, some became good friends and others just acquaintances. She referred to them as angels among men. There were a few that left a stamp on her heart. Many even came to her to have their hair done when she was unable to travel; they didn't have to but they did because they cared about her.

In Rose's early years of struggle, she met a friend called Meredith, who was of Caribbean heritage, humble, Rose thought her a perfect human being. She had a certain presence about her that one noticed immediately. She had puppy -dog eyes that Rose would tease her about. A pure soul who had so much to give, she was well spoken, and her manners were of a high standard. They met while Rose, was working in Huntingdon. Meredith had never worn a hair weave, but Rose convinced her that she could create one in such away, it would look natural. It was a funny conversation and in the end she decided to give it a go. Meredith and Rose became close friends over the years, and she would often travel to London to see Rose. She had everything – a fantastic job, a home, and a husband but deep down she wasn't happy. Sometimes she would complain of the ill treatment that she had to endure from her husband, and eventually she lost her job due to the constant ridicule from her boss. "Why do you allow people to treat you so horribly," Rose demanded. All she did was cry. Wiping her tears she said,

"I don't want to get anyone into trouble". After several years she resigned her job. The sparkle she had was disappearing slowly; her husband left her after twenty years. It was difficult for her, and Rose watching her slipping away, begged Meredith to get professional help. It wasn't easy watching someone suffer in such harsh and mean way. She would come around less and less and then she was gone. For years Rose tried to find her, even the phone number that she once used was no longer available. Rose hoped that one day, they`d see each other again, yet that didn't happen. People come and they go. Rose wondered what life would`ve been like if they'd stayed around. Meredith was a big part of her life for a while, and not knowing what happened to her and if she ever sorted herself out made her heart ache; she never stopped thinking about her.

After all his years of overindulgence with alcohol Rose's father became a new man, giving his life to God, and he started attending church with their mom. For many years she remembered praying for him to change and now it was here. When they were children that would've been an absolute miracle for them. Some people believe that God doesn't always come through; Rose's mother always said that God is an untimely God, and that had been an essential part of their lives. Her religious beliefs were something that she lived by, teaching the children to pray at a young age, learning to read the bible and attending church. Rose had questioned The Creator's presence for years, because she did not get the results she has been asking for. 'Hmmm, he did come through after all,' she thought to herself smiling and nodding her head, looking out the of the plain glass window of the flat she shared with her partner.

Jenna too had gotten her own place, and was living with her daughter in the area she was familiar with. Rose had moved around to some degree, but it didn't stop she and her sister from seeing each other. They'd talk every day on the phone, though, like they'd never left.

"Sis, you heard the good news? Papa's been baptised. Isn't that amazing?" she pauses on the phone, waiting to hear her sister's response. "God is good but it's been a long time coming." You should have heard them laughing, it was like getting a birthday present, something that they'd never thought they would get. The next day Rose called home, congratulating her dad on his triumphant accomplishment.

" I'm proud of you, papa," Rose told him happily.

212

"Well my daughter, it's time for changes and I`m not getting any younger." They talked for a while, then Rose asked to speak to her mother, who sounded blissfully happy; she could almost see her face over the phone. Unfortunately, Rose's father became unwell, and so he visited his doctor to find out what was happening to him. He did test after test, and eventually they found out that he had stage three prostate cancer.

Poor papa was devastated; he wasn't afraid of dying but was scared of the agonising deterioration and not being able to help himself – that was his worst fear. It was a difficult time for everyone; having no health insurance the expense of each visit was also weighing heavily upon him. Rose and Jenna assisted him as much as they could, but he was also a proud man and taking money from his children bruised his ego. The doctors knew that he had no chance surviving, but never told him that, instead continuing bleeding him dry. He wasn't recovering, no matter how much money he paid, and he was getting weaker every day; some days were worse than others. None of the past was important now, and thank God he was given a second chance to redeem himself. He was an authentic man; regardless of his flaws he had good values even though it took years for Rose to acknowledge it, she finally saw the good in him. It was sad to hear his voice not knowing, how long he had, and was harder for Rose and her sister who weren't able to see or visit him. Talking to him on the phone, required putting him first, sounding as cheerful as possible, distracting him with stories about England, the weather and anything else. But then there were days when he wanted to talk about his illness and pains, and Rose had to respect that. He was truly brave, and often his agony was plain to hear. Rose and Jenna were calling almost every day. Del was there accompanying him to his appointments, everyone who was there with him did their part.

The darkness was still lingering; you could hear the vehicles accelerating at speed, and be able to differentiate between the sounds of a bus or something smaller. People were now walking the street going about their business, the streetlights were now off leaving, natural brightness at its best. It was early morning and Rose had just got out of bed, when suddenly her mobile rang. Looking at the incoming call, it wasn't local but from back home. It was rather strange for anyone to be calling that early in the morning.

"Hello she answered in an uncertain tone,

"Yes Rose, you heard the news that your old man died a couple hours ago in the hospital.

"What," Rose screamed in horror; she wasn't sure if she heard correctly. Rose's dad was at Maria's house spending some time with them when he felt ill and was taken to the local hospital where after a few days, he died. They said that he didn't suffer, and passed away peacefully. There was great lamentation following his death. Rose's mother was heartbroken and so was everyone else. His body was moved back to a funeral home, closer to home. Rose was unable to travel, and so was Jenna and that was more unbearable than one could imagine. Luckily for Rose and her sister they had some money saved away, and they made sure he had a proper send off, and other family members were supportive, too, and did their part.

After he was buried, then came the silent Willy to hold the fort; he was now responsible for the cultivated fields, amongst other things. He was the only one who managed all their father's fields, plus attending to his own. /the older brothers weren't inclined to help, and whenever they did, Willy would have to pay them. He worked as hard to maintain the farms as its their father had, and he did a great job. Life after Rose's dad had passed away was difficult, especially for their mother, but she had family and friends supporting her. Rose felt heavy-hearted at losing a man who had once been an enemy, and then became her beloved father. She needed more time, but his life was cut short. Sam was affected deeply, having been close to his granddad.

Life was getting back on track after months for everyone, but Rose's mom was still trying to cope with his death. Three years after Rose's papa's death she and her sister went back home to visit their family for the first time in many years. It was a magnificent moment, and the happiest Rose had been in years, seeing her boys again, who she hadn't seen in almost a decade. Neil had grown so tall and handsome and followed his mother everywhere that she went; it was like old times. With Sam it was slightly different because he wasn't as attached as his brother. After a few days their bond grew stronger, and she filled them with hugs and kisses; they went everywhere together. They were no strangers; to Rose had made sure of that by talking to them almost every day while she'd been away. Rose and Jenna spent their time between the houses of Del, Maria and the home they had lived in for many years. Willy lived close to home, so it was no trouble seeing them all.

It was time to return to England; saying goodbye was more excruciating than Rose had anticipated, reminding her of when she had left before, but this time it was different. The day came, and most of the family went including Rose's boys. They talked and laughed throughout the journey to Kingston. Rose promised Sam and Neil that they'd see her soon, but it was decided that it was best they continue their education back home. Rose didn't have the facilities and funding to take them. Rose commented that they would have the best education, something that she never had. She carried a melancholy sadness with her because she was unable to take them as she had originally had hoped, her aim wasn't to fail them again. Coming back, Rose worked harder than ever, fulfilling her obligations and for years that's what she did. Rose did return a few years after, spending time with her family and bonding closer with her sons. She went on putting herself through school, so that she could obtained a better job. Rose's mind worked, on impulse, always wanting to learn, and so she pushed herself, sometimes to the limit. Rose was now back in London, with her son. Jenna was getting on with life as normal, but this wasn't the end of their anguish and suffering, something unexpected was about to happen.

They say that death has no favourites, and it doesn't respect, nor have regards, for any man, and that has been a constant reminder on evidence throughout the years. Ms Peg who was once the survivor of many robberies, who suffered much embarrassment over her husband after he had consumed a few red stripe beers. She finally lost her battle with womb cancer and passed away. Rose was very sad about the news, even though they didn't really keep in contact with each other, except through Pauline; she and Rose communicated whenever they were able to. When Ms Peg died, the business went with her because no one else was equally to running it. It wasn't long after that Buggy came to his demised; the thing that he had loved for so many years became his curse. Pauline told Rose that he had being drinking heavily during the day, mounted his motorbike went riding as he had been doing for years. Buggy was knocked off his motorbike by a car, he was badly fractured, and died because from serious head injuries. Losing one parent is hard enough, but two following behind each other one must have a significant support base. Pauline was always smart, when it came to saving; initially she was the first person who took Rose into a bank to open her account. Things went downhill for a time, but she managed to stay afloat, even under the horrible circumstances. She had four children of her own but was never married, she was literally a single mother.

It was four years since Rose's dad was buried and resting in peace; people often talked about him like he wasn't never dead . Last time Rose had seen Willy, they had bonded very well and no matter how messed up life seemed they remained together. He was a fantastic father and husband to his family (they had two sons), but farming was hard work, toiling away trying to make ends meet. Most of the earnings went to into the fields, paying his workers and maintaining the fields, sometimes the crops were cheap, but they managed. Everyone had their own life; for some it was taking its strain, others appeared lost, a few kept fighting for redemption.

One day Rose was getting ready for work, her son already having gone to school when the phone rang, a harbinger of bad news, Rose glanced at the incoming number and saw it was her nephew Kevin. They'd always kept in touch, and she'd assisted him whenever she could. 'Why would he be calling me so early,' Rose thought feeling like her stomach was going to erupt " Hello nephew," Rose addressed him, "what's going on? Is everything ok?

He sounded empty like someone had pulled his insides out.

"Did you hear the news?" he said slowly

Rose's hands were shaking, so she sat down on the bed, breathing deeply.

"They murdered Willy."

"What, when how?" She couldn't make much sense of what Kevin was saying. Rose screamed out her hopelessness. She felt weak and was unable to move. How could this be? It wasn't possible. My God! She felt the blood in her body freeze. Kevin went on to explain what he had heard leading up to the murder; it was heart- breaking to listen to and after he hung up the phone she wept bitterly.

When their father died it was shocking but expected in some harsh way, but no one could ever have believed that such a spine-chilling crime as this could have happened to their family. Rose found herself at the bottom of her stairs, inside her house but wasn't sure how she got there. As she sat there weeping Rose heard a knocking on her door; she didn't respond but then,

"Rose, are you OK," shouted her neighbour from outside. She then opened the door and let her in; weeping was all she was able to do, nothing made sense. The neighbour did her best to console Rose, but that was impossible, and she watched helplessly, not knowing what to do. She was going to work but begged Rose to call her if she needed anything, and Rose looked at her and nodded her head.

It was late evening Rose was told by his wife, and it was unusual for him to not be at home. Earlier they had heard a sound like an explosion; they were unsure what it was because the noise was unfamiliar to them. the community has never had such unlawful act. When he didn't come home they went in search of him, asking anyone if they'd seen him earlier in the evening. One person said that they saw him going towards the path that led to the forest. His son was walking ahead of the others, and so was unfortunately the first to see his lifeless body lying curled up in the dirt, having bled to death. He was gunned down and left for dead alone and terrified. The hardest part of him being murdered was that nobody knew why, and that remained a mystery for many years.

Nothing was ever the same, and his poor son was traumatized for days after he found his father's body. It was the biggest horror the family had ever suffered, and everyone was solemnly affected. Rose and Jenna were lost, grief stricken; the pain was unbearable, especially as they weren't able to attend his funeral. Rose's mother was in shock for days and everyone was scared for her well-being. His wife and children lost a father and a husband, a provider, and a friend; on one should go through such extreme suffering. Rose and Jenna had only come back a few months before, so they weren't able to return on such short notice. The cycle had returned, it was the same thing they had done for their beloved dad, assisting with their brother wasn't any different. He would never be forgotten; he had so much to give but someone decided that taking his life was their duty. Eventually the suspect was held, and was in jail for four years, then was released due to lack of evidence. He was never given a sentence, just walked away like he did nothing. Rose's mother took it hard after hearing that the killer was released, and to this day it still affects her. It took a while adjusting back to normality, but what does that really mean for those who must carry that burden with them every day. His children are now adult and teenager, getting on with life as best they can. They remain determined, regardless of the odds, in making their lives progressive and successful even though they face many endeavours along the way.

Today Jenna is now living life to the fullest with her daughter, who has a challenging condition, but given the assistance that she receives life gets easier, although her struggles will last a lifetime. Jenna and Rose's bond of sisterhood and friendship has endured the test of time. Making them an unstoppable force to reckon with; nothing has changed between them. Del now has two children; one is a teenager and the other is an adult, and she is doing well for herself, living oversea with her husband. Kevin emigrated with his daughter, the most dedicated father Rose had ever known; he works hard, and one day soon he will be victorious. Kelly, Rose's niece, who grew up with them like a sister, has been married for years ,and still lives with her family. She is also a successful teacher, mother and a dedicated Christian. Maria is now a widow after losing her husband, Ricky, to a terrible disease that he had being fighting with for years. Rose remained in touch with Diane and her family throughout the years. Neil and Sam are now adults too, and both were given the same opportunities. Sam has graduated from college, but is still searching for something, not sure what he's looking for. Rose continues to encourage him, hoping that one day he might find his true path. Neil and his mother remain close he's pursuing his dreams and is still attending university. Rose and her sisters devoted their lives to taking care of their mother, who still resides at the family home, A most wonderful mother and a great supporter towards her children.

Rose has been living with her partner and husband for over eighteen years, and they have two sons together. She is a dedicated mother, supportive and motivated towards positive change. She teaches her children to believe in themselves, no matter what, loving and living life to its fullness. She has always said, 'what is life without challenges?' It's what give us the strength, not giving up, but to carry on, reaching for the stars. Rose now wants to pursue a career in being a writer and novelist. She will also begin her studies in Creative Writing (BA) at Birkbeck university in London. After all every dark cloud has a silver lining.